'Chissick writes with an intensity of feeling and compassion for her characters . . . The narrative is couched in highly impressionistic prose . . . The language is elaborately poetic, the overall effect intoxicating enough to leave the impression that *Colourbook* is a work of some definite literary significance'
The Times

'Written in extremely accessible but very sparse prose, Rosalyn Chissick's second novel is as haunting, thrilling and memorable as her first . . . An unforgettable book'
Shine

'What makes the book so powerful is its reluctance to hold anyone culpable for what ensues'
Big Issue

'The words used are beautiful, harsh realities softened with lyrical rhythms'
Bath Chronicle

'The writing has a cinematic quality'
Bristol Evening Post

Colourbook

ROSALYN CHISSICK

SCEPTRE

Copyright © 1999 by Rosalyn Chissick

First published in 1999 by Hodder and Stoughton
This edition published in 2000 by Hodder and Stoughton
A division of Hodder Headline
A Sceptre Paperback

10 9 8 7 6 5 4 3 2 1

A CIP catalogue record for this book is
available from the British Library.

ISBN 0 340 70781 X

Printed and bound in Great Britain by
Mackays of Chatham PLC, Chatham Kent

Hodder and Stoughton
A division of Hodder Headline
338 Euston Road
London NW1 3BH

for my grandmothers:
Ethel Davis and Ray Chissick

'Look at this for the benefit of All with loving kindness and compassion.'

Shola Gyurme
(Chol-pa Lama)

thank you and love

to: Alyson Hallett

and to: Michael Chissick, Murray Groves, Elisabeth Winkler, Mercedes Catton, Tricia Wastvedt, Nick Morgan, Lindsey Woloski, Melanie Yudolph, Louise Hart, Fatina Cummings. And Ludwig.

Contents

Contents

harbour

He says his name is Joe, holding a dead fish out to her. It has a rainbow on its back. Milk-white fins and a tail.

Rainy sea port. Tables and chairs anchored under tarpaulin and black plastic that flaps in the wind like birds.

He saw her standing in the alleyway.

Joe.

Wanting to keep her there.

He takes her to a pub. First pub she has ever been inside. Fire in the corner casting orange shadows over the sawdust and concrete floor. Men sitting on chairs round barrels.

Marie shreds her first beer mat. Sips her first rum. All the time thinking about her second.

You're too young to be in here, he says.

I'm not.

Got a boyfriend?

Maybe.

Anyone special?

No.

She is pretty sitting there. Pretty and out of place.

Still at school?

No.

What do you do then?

I work in an office.

An office? He looks directly at her.

I type, she says, looking directly back at him. I type letters and answer the phone. I would like another drink, she says.

He cooks the fish on a charcoal fire on the harbour. Passing chunks to her on a fork. Tastes of smoke and seaweed. They share a large apple pie and drink tea out of tin mugs.

He says: I'm going to get carried away with you.

She likes the thought of him being carried away with her, so caught up in her that he loses his reason, his mind, his—

Self-control, he says. You expect me to have self-control. And all the time you sit there baiting me.

Baiting you?

You're a worm on a hook and I am the fish. The big, ravenous fish.

He kisses her and her shoe gets caught in the nets left there to dry. The crunch of shells underfoot.

One of these day, he says.

And she says: what's wrong with now?

Now?

He never expected that from her. Thought she was teasing when all the time she—

Are you sure?

Yes, she says.

Stumbling through the dark after him.

Hold my hand, he says.

It is rough and callused.

He smells of beer and sea water. Up close, his jacket is slimy with oil.

Stumbling on to his boat and he lights a lamp with a match.

Follow me. Be quiet.

Lantern swinging in front of her and down into his cabin.

There is a photograph of a woman by his bed. He turns it to face the wall.

Who is she?

She is no one. No one for you to worry about. Come here.

He is rough with her. One minute tender and loving—

pretty little baby, smooth skin, he says, nice.

Then he is pawing at her, hands so rough and fast that they—

Wanting to say: stop it.

And then: are you protected?

Protected?

He comes on her chest and it splashes in her face.

Mopping at puddles of blood and semen with his T-shirt.

Saying: are you all right to stay the night?

No, she says, struggling back into her underwear. Knickers, bra, tights now with ladders. I've got to go home, they will be worried.

It was your first time.

Yes, she says.

Will I see you again?

Marie nods.

Marie likes sneaking out of her room at night to run down to the harbour to see him. Likes making a hump in her bed out of jumpers and a coat, in case her parents look in to check up on her. Lipstick in her purse, her mother's perfume, her best friend's heels.

She brings him cheese and meat from her parents' fridge. One night she takes his clothes home to wash and tells her mother they belong to a friend's father.

His wife's in hospital, she says. I'm washing his clothes to help them out.

Lathering up Joe's trousers, shirts and holey socks in the kitchen sink. Inhaling his smells. Wanting to be doing this for him for the rest of her life. Then one day he might take her to sea. Instead of the harbour they might make love on the waves.

It gets better. She starts to touch his body and although she is not sure what to do he guides her and says:

Yes, that's right, you're a natural.

She has found something she is good at so she tries harder all the time.

The feel of him inside her. Not always so fast and rough now. And sometimes he calls out her name.

Marie.

Yes.

Do you want to try it like this?

Twisting her body into knots. And so many sensations.

One day, she says, when we are married—

And he drops her out of his arms like she is hot, white hot.

When we're what?

She says the words again: when we're married.

Where did you get that idea?

His arms shake, as if she is still inside them and he will not be able to get her out.

When did I ever say—?

She says quietly: you didn't.

Lighting a cigarette, orange tip flaring into the darkness.

Already got a wife, Joe says.

And Marie feels small; ugly and small. Turning round the photograph on the shelf by his bed to see a yellow-haired woman standing at the entrance to a tent.

A circus tent?

Yes.

Your wife?

Yes.

She turns the photograph over, looking at its dirty white back and a ring-stain of tea where, perhaps, Joe rested his cup. But she can still see his wife's face. Her name – Helen – and a message – love always – scribbled across the back in red ink.

Joe is not saying anything, sitting at the other end of the bed with his hands stiff and still upon his thighs.

Then, as gently as he can, he says: you are special.

Special?

Feeling the word sticky as an old boiled sweet.

Yes, a special, lovely girl. You deserve better, he says.

Fareport – Marie reads the word on the back of the photograph. Is that where she's from?

Who?

Your wife.

Yes, says Joe. Us – we—

It's where you live.

Yes.

Suddenly knowing the words to use, remembering the ones that stop the tears. That's the main thing. Stop her from crying and trying to hold on.

Seeing the knots she is making with her fingers, shoulders slumping towards him.

He says: one day, when this is all over—

Over?

Yes, he says, over.

And now she is crying. Dabbing at her eyes with a corner of the sheet.

Please don't cry.

Straightening up, Marie feels suddenly naked. Cold and naked. Reaching on to the floor for her dress and thick fingers struggling with the buttons.

Watching her, red in the face, Joe says: shall I help you
with that?

Fastening buttons, touching her skin with the back of
his hand.

Then she is turning around and holding on to him. Arms
around his shoulders, his bare chest next to her dress. She
sees the line of hairs spiralling across his shoulders, the back
of his shoulders where she is resting her hands. He does not
move but he does not push her away and she is sobbing now
into his hair.

I'm sorry, he says.

Peeling her body away from his, standing up, smoothing
her hair, running a hand across each eye. As Marie stands
by the door the boat rocks, lifting her up and then down,
carrying her on a wave.

She hears herself saying: thank you, as she undoes the bolt
on his door.

At night, still, Marie goes down to the harbour to look at the
boat and peer in the windows of the pub. One night one of
Joe's friends spots her, standing in the shadows.

Coming in? he asks, holding the door open for her.

But she shakes her head.

Looking for Joe?

No, she says, yes.

He's back at the boat. You sure you won't come in for
a drink?

Walking back, hearing only the slap of water against the harbour side, the hiss and gurgle of boats. Imagining Joe missing her but trapped by the circumstances of his life. Maybe he married too young, before he knew what love was. Perhaps it's love he feels for Marie. Maybe he's thinking about her right now.

Clattering on to the boat and swaying towards his cabin. Seeing the light under the door. The pungent smell of his tobacco.

The door is unlocked. Joe is sitting on his bed, listening to the radio.

Marie says: I don't mind that you are married. All I want is to be with you. It's all right – that you have a wife. I don't mind.

But I do.

He wishes she had not come. Wishes he had gone to the pub with the others. His head aches.

She is sitting opposite him on the bed now, one hand crawling across the sheet towards him.

Marie, it's over.

It can't be.

She touches his fingers and he does not recoil. Uncurls, instead, in front of her. Lifting his head first, then his chest, straightening his back until she can see the whole of him.

She looks very pretty. In her grey coat with big silver buttons. She is wearing coral-coloured lipstick. There are blue lines around her eyes. He wants to be alone and yet –

he remembers the tight smoothness of her body. She is asking for him again. He cannot think of a reason to say no.

If you're sure this is what you want, he says.

She says: I want to be with you.

When Joe's boat leaves, he says that he will write to her. Standing on the harbour shielding his eyes from the sun. She asks for his address and he says:

It's not a good idea. My wife—

Yes, of course.

But I'll write.

Will you?

Yes, he says. And I'll be back.

Do you promise?

Life is uncertain, he says. You never totally know.

Waiting for Joe's letter.

Racing to the box when she hears the postman.

One day asking him: is that all?

All?

No more post for this house?

He checks his bag again.

No, that's it for this morning. Waiting for a letter are you? He laughs. All I do, he says, is the delivering. If a man doesn't write, he says pointedly, to his sweetheart, there's not a lot I can do.

Three days of sickness
  Three nights when she cannot sleep.
  She sees Joe's wife's face and always she is laughing.
  Marie goes to the chemist and buys a pregnancy test. The woman puts the box in a bag slowly, noisily. Asks for the money dangling the bag just out of Marie's reach.

Locked in her parents' bathroom, Marie is waiting for the colour to show. Seeing purple although the strip is as blue as her jumper. Running to the window and seeing blue.

blue eyes in a
long
pink face

Sam has dreams of becoming an academic, someone others will come to and share the wrestlings of their minds. Ah, he will say, I know the answer to that, and he will sort them all out with the things that he knows.

His father is going to be proud of him. Stiff old man in a battered brown suit. First one in the family to go away to college.

Make us proud of you son, he says.

Smiling at him, cuffing him. Mussing up his hair so Sam feels unkempt as he gets on to the train. Sitting with the other boys and their shiny newness. Polished boots; jackets and bags. Rows and rows of them all gleaming. And his father on the train until the last minute. Checking a hundred meaningless things.

Have you got a clean handkerchief?

Of course I have father.

His mother crying on the platform in her pale green coat. Straightening Sam's tie and the other boys are watching.

Don't worry about me father.

I've given you everything.

Hearing the whistle.

Now it's up to you.

Sam thinks of his father when he rises in the morning, throughout the day and then last thing at night. Am I working hard enough? Do I fully understand what I am learning? I will put in an extra half-day at the library tomorrow. I need to get good grades.

And everywhere, pretty girls away from their parents. Standing in groups on corners and at bus stops. All around him as he queues at the canteen. Girls in citrus-coloured jumpers: lemon, lime and orange. Hawking thin skirts over their knees and twiddling pencils, writing in books, looking out of windows, occasionally looking at him.

And he looks away. Because he is here to learn and girls are a distraction. Learning comes first, his father says.

In the library, a girl passes Sam an invitation for her party. Over the pile of books between them. All he can see is the card and her braceleted hand.

Will you come?

She stands up and he can see her brown hair and dark eyes.

When is it?

Saturday. It's for my birthday. Please say you will come.

And for the next few hours, instead of his father, he sees the face of the girl in the library. She said her name was Lauren.

Sam's father telephones as he is getting ready to go to the party.

Working hard are you son?

Yes, says Sam. Every minute.

Well, don't forget to have some fun.

And Sam feels suddenly as if his evening is being sanctioned.

There's a party tonight, he falters, I'm going out.

There is a silence and Sam wishes he had not told him. His father's voice is monotone when he eventually speaks.

That's fine son. You make me proud.

The music is thumping. Sam can't see the girl from the library, but there are so many others. Finds himself standing next to a girl in a black wool dress. She is swaying to the music, her thigh intermittently knocking against his.

Do you want to dance?

She has not heard him.

Impossible to ask her again, to shout above the music, to make her turn round and see him.

I will dance with you.

A skinny girl standing on his other side. There is lipstick on her teeth. Makes her look bizarrely like she is bleeding.

Sam follows her, weaving between groups of people, catching snatches of their talk.

The girl moves swiftly. Movements small and jerky.

What's your name?

She has to come close so he can hear her.

Marie, she says.

Blue eyes in a long pink face.

His hands are delicate, smooth as paper, dry hand in dry hand, following his careful, even steps.

He tells her he wants to be a scientist, make a new discovery. Asks: what do you want?

Marie can think of nothing. Nothing except Joe's baby in her belly.

Smiling at the chemistry student, at the tired green tweed of his lapel.

Marie has a bottle of rum in her bag and she takes Sam into the corner to swig from it. It burns his throat and then the heat floods his body.

By the time he finds Lauren, they have run out of rum. Marie's fingers inside his, Marie huddling closer to him (she feels warm through her dress), Marie kissing him in front of Lauren. And Sam feels a tightness in his belly watching Lauren move away.

Marie wants to come with him, back to his room.

She says: I like you. I like, she leans against him, your shyness. The way you run out of words. She laughs. Then string hundreds together all at once.

Marie finds a taxi, an off-licence, money in Sam's pocket, his keys.

Saying: which room is yours? and running ahead of him to unlock the door.

Get some glasses.

Dispensing orders from the centre of his bed. She throws a scarf over the lampshade, rearranges the books on the bedside table.

Won't be needing these, she says and a book falls to the floor with a clatter.

Sam stoops to pick it up and she is laughing.

Or am I making a mistake? she asks. Is it your books you want to be with tonight?

Sam takes another gulp of rum. Sitting on the bed beside Marie. So close he can feel her breath on his face.

The first time Sam kisses Marie, his father's face is in front of him so strongly it is as if he is kissing his father. Opening his eyes and pulling back from her.

What's the matter? she asks. Don't you like me?

He puts his hand on her breast and it feels warm.

Do you mind?

No, she whispers, why should I?

Clenching her teeth in the darkness, moving her hand into his lap.

And kissing her again. The feel of her hands, the feel of her body. Sam thinks: I want a corner of my life without my father. A corner just for myself.

Gasping on top of her. Knowing it all happened too quickly but there was no way he could have stopped it. Rolling away from her. Pushing his nose against the wall.

Don't worry, Marie says.

And she puts her arm around his back.

It's all right, she says.

Waking next to Marie. Sam barely breathes in case he should disturb her. Four a.m. The light is pink in the room, the dusty pink of her scarf and he looks at her arm curled on top of the sheet, the skin of her fingers, her shoulder, her throat. It is several minutes before he thinks of his father and linked to that thought, like a foot on the end of a leg, is the thought of the night before. Several cities between them and the old man has a hold still, like he is here in this room.

Wanting to lose himself, his thoughts, his father, in the girl beside him. It ought to be possible, Sam thinks. Starting to stroke Marie.

Six weeks later Marie moves in, filling Sam's bedsit, his head, his life.

Telling his father: Sam is out, when he calls; although Sam is sitting next to her on the couch. She puts her finger over his lips, sounds so serious, talking to his father, but smiling. Looking at Sam and smiling.

Yes, I will tell him that you rang. When he gets back from the library. But it may be late.

Sam feels guilty – guilty that his books lie unread and his assignment is late, guilty about his father, his poor father, after all he has done. But Sam is happy. Absurdly happy.

He fails his chemistry test.

The tutor says: what is happening Sam?

What do you mean sir?

You started out well, now you are lagging.

Sam hangs his head because the tutor has the voice of his father. His father saying: don't fail me son. His father wanting to feel proud.

When his father says: I'm coming for a visit,

Sam tells Marie: you'd better stay away.

Why? she asks. Are you ashamed of me?

No, he says. It's not like that.

What if I was pregnant?

Pregnant?

The word sounds strange to him as he speaks it, unfamiliar.

You said you're on the pill.

I am, she says. But it's not a hundred per cent safe.

Sam read a leaflet about it once, they guarantee ninety per cent, or is it eighty? Not odds worth worrying about. Not with his father due in a few hours. Rearranging the books on his table, gathering together Marie's clothing scattered across the chair.

You have to go.

She is at the door and he is pushing her, gently.

What if she loses him, she thinks suddenly, after all her work?

I am, she says quietly.

Am what?

Sam is picking a coffee cup off the floor, he is looking at his watch.

Pregnant, she says. With your child.

The next hours are a blur to Sam. He passes out on the floor, comes round with his head on Marie's lap and his father standing there, looking at a text book on his table.

What happens to matter at absolute zero?

All motion ceases, says Sam. It becomes perfectly still.

And the molecular geometry of NI3, says his father – tell me what is that?

Sam vomits over his shoes.

And her? he whispers, because Marie is in the kitchen and they are alone together at last.

Her name is Marie.

I know. I asked you, who is she? Is she your girlfriend?

Yes.

And? Marie is standing in the doorway holding a tray piled with cups and saucers. He is afraid she will drop the tray, her voice is rising. Sam, what am I?

He feels the walls of the room running at him again.

You tell me, Marie. His father turns to her. What else are you?

Soon to be, she looks at her shoes—

Soon to be, says Sam, my bride.

He did not have to search for the word, it was as if it had always been there. Bride. From the moment she told him she was pregnant. No, before that, from the moment she took him inside. There were never going to be any great adventures.

His father's anger.

And Marie, on the sofa, crying.

I'm sorry, she says. I'm sorry.

But she does not mention the baby and so, thinks Sam, with our secrecy comes the beginnings of a bond.

Sam would hate Marie but he does not have the energy. Besides, he has the rest of his life to hate her, hate her and the rest of his life.

———————

Sam's father does not come to the wedding. His mother sends a letter, tiny, squashed together words in almost transparent blue ink.

Your father will not let me come. But my loving heart is with you.

Pink and blue hotel with a dirty white awning. Round tables in the garden. A help-yourself notice behind the bar.

We pride ourselves on our lack of formality, says the owner. You are family when inside of our house.

Showing Marie and Sam to a room with a view of the sea. Yellow and purple flowers. Newly-weds welcome, strung in paper letters across the bed.

Be happy, she trills, as she closes the door behind her.

And to Sam, it sounds like a command: be happy. Like they might be. Like they have a chance.

When Sam falls asleep, Marie walks down the hall to the payphone, dials her parents' number.

Are there any letters for me? she whispers

She waits while her mother rustles through the pile of papers by the telephone.

There is a postcard, says her mother.

A postcard?

With a picture of a palm tree.

Who is it from?

Waiting while her mother deciphers.

It's signed Jon, her mother reads it to her.

Joe?

There is a pause. I suppose it could be.

What does it say?

Dear Marie.

Her mother coughs.

I am thinking about you.

There is a pause.

And? says Marie into the silence.

And? says her mother.

Is that all?

Just that, she says at last, and the sender's name.

Her mother reads it again – Jon.

Feeling violently and so helplessly angry with her mother, for being so—

Stupid. How can you be so stupid? It's Joe. Joe. Joe.

And each time Marie says his name her voice rises a little higher until she is shouting Joe into the corridor and a woman in a dressing gown comes to her door, puts a finger to her lips.

Such a quick marriage thinks Marie's mother, putting the telephone back on the hook. Lucky Marie to get Sam. Lucky Marie's mother to have someone take Marie off her hands. It was a relief, she lets this thought slip through like a small boat on a lazy river. A relief to hand Marie on to someone else.

Sam hears Marie's voice in the hall. Wakes to the sound of her calling Joe.

Who's Joe?

She is barely inside the door and he is staggering to his feet.

Another lover?

Marie says: don't be silly.

I'll bet – he coughs out the words he has not yet spoken – I bet it's not my baby.

Not your baby?

Marie starts to cry. Head in her hands, shoulders heaving.

And he is sorry, immediately repentant, trying to hold her.

Marie, I'm sorry. I didn't mean it. I'm drunk, I'm sorry.

Do you think I wanted to trap you?

No, he says. No.

Do you think so little of me?

I think the world of you, he says, you're my wife.

Sam does not mention it again. But now he has said it – not my baby – he cannot take it back. It occupies a box in his head with a lid that won't stay down. The thought popping out at him when he least expects it – not your baby – when he is cleaning his teeth – not your baby – in the bathroom, not your baby, when they are making love – not your baby – and Marie is calling his name.

Marie gets a job in a sweet shop.

Eating for two, she says, although it looks like four.

So many pretty women in the streets, on the buses, serving behind counters. Sam had thought he would get to know a few of them. Not just one.

Not just one.

Writing to his father: Marie is going to have a baby. Will you come to see your grandchild?

His mother writes back: your father is still very angry. Give him time – I cannot say how long – he put all his hope in you. Why did you let him down?

Sam never expected such joy.

Holding his daughter for the first time.

Tiny, curled up thing.

He had not imagined such minute fingers, such soft skin, such perfect toes.

Our daughter.

Putting the words together for the first time.

And Marie in a pink dressing gown, smoothing the sheet with her fingers.

You like her?

How could anyone not like her?

Flooded with a new feeling for Marie. Wanting to hold and stroke her hand.

Walking up and down with their daughter, Pia, while Marie is sleeping. Finding himself speaking secrets into her downy head.

Sam thinks about Pia every hour. Telephones Marie several times a day to ask how she is.

She's fine, says Marie. Don't you want to know how I am?

Of course.

I'm fat and I'm lonely.

Sam buys Marie chocolates with almond centres. She bites into one and says: I prefer them soft.

She likes strawberry cream, orange, coffee, soft white mint. Fondant centres. Running her finger across the top of a cake to coat it in icing. Stirring sugar into her tea. Honey on her toast in the morning and late at night.

I can't help it, she says when she catches him staring at her. You don't know what it's like. Stuck here day after day.

Maire befriends another mother. They put their babies in pushchairs and take them to a department store. They try on hats and coats and rings, get sprayed with perfume, comment on the season's colours as they change. A new pink lipstick, a blusher called hint of exotica.

Terracotta, says the salesgirl. All the fashion, all the rage.

Purchases packaged in smart red bags. Then up the escalator to the cafeteria. Looking at the dessert trolley and wanting to taste everything.

Asking for: Black Forest gateau, happy that the slice selected boasts two glacé cherries.

Extra cream? asks the waitress.

Yes, says Marie. And – as the waitress turns to leave – will you bring me another hot chocolate?

Certainly, says the waitress. Would you like a flake with that?

It's not fair, thinks Sam, squashed into a corner of the sofa by Marie. Pudgy arms under his nose, her fat legs curled up underneath her like the roots of a tree. It's not fair, thinks Sam – and he can feel his bottom lip pouting – not fair for a woman to look one way when you marry her and to look completely different within a few months. Not even a year since he met her and she has totally let herself go.

Looking at the television guide, hoping he will see the schedule has changed.

He picks up a book, but Marie starts to fidget.

Is that so much more interesting to be with than me?

When Pia wakes and starts crying, Sam feels relieved. Is about to stand up, but Marie's hand is on his arm.

Let her cry. The doctors say it's good for them. We shouldn't be always at her beck and call. She will grow up spoilt, says Marie. Always wanting her own way.

Sam wriggles out of Marie's grasp and walks towards the bedroom. He touches Pia and she is quiet. Suddenly, wonderfully. It feels to him like a small miracle. Each time he picks his daughter up and she is calmed.

the
conductor

Joe's boat docks and he telephones Marie's parents.

Her mother tells him: Marie has gone.

And he says: all right then, it doesn't matter.

But Marie's mother says: I can give you a number for her.

And he has no one else to see here, no other plans, nothing much to do, so he says: okay, why not?

He does not call Marie for three days and when he does it is because he has a hangover and he has been imagining the feel of a woman's fingers trailing across his forehead.

Marie.

Yes?

She is holding Pia with one arm, the telephone wedged into the shoulder of the other.

Hello Marie. Guess who it is.

She says: Joe, almost before he gets to the end of his sentence and there is a silence because he is caught off guard. Didn't expect to be remembered so instantly.

Are you busy?

The words come out in a staccato.

Right now? she says. No.

Do you feel like coming to see me on the boat?

Words more easy now, but still the throbbing in his temples.

It has been over a year, she says at last, since I heard from you.

Don't you want to come?

I'll be there in an hour, she says.

Marie dresses Pia in white. Ties a bow in her hair. Wants her to look perfect – wiping a smudge away from the side of her mouth but she does it roughly, with a corner of a tea towel and Pia starts to cry, tears running in lines down her face.

Stop it, says Marie. Stop it now.

But the baby just cries more, scrunching up her entire face.

Marie shakes her. Just once. Holding Pia by the shoulders and lifting her up off the bed. Almost before the movement is over, Marie stops cold, hands clamped around the small shape of her daughter. She feels as if the hands are not her own. Drops Pia very gently on to the bed.

Standing back from the bed, back from her still crying daughter, eventually Marie reaches out a hand and smoothes Pia's tangled hair.

Marie is trying on her favourite clothes, in descending order. Fumbling with zips that won't fasten and bits of cloth that won't meet.

Seeing fat when she looks at herself in the mirror.

Seeing fat as she rouges her cheeks and backcombs her hair.

The bus does not arrive for ages and Marie has to stand at the bus stop with an old woman who keeps squinting at her watch.

Bus should have been here ten minutes ago.

Yes, says Marie.

Twelve minutes late now.

Holding the small gold watch close to her crêpey eyelids.

Fourteen, nearly fifteen minutes late now. I'm going to be late.

Late, the word eats up Marie's mind – but at least she does not know the exact time.

Four fifteen, says the woman. I'm going to be very, very late.

Eventually seeing the bus and how slowly it crawls from a distant speck, to stopping here in front of them. How slowly the old woman moves up the stairs, how thick-fingered the conductor counting out her change.

Marie points out trees to Pia as they drive along. At one junction a marmalade cat and a Pekingese scowling. Anything to pass the yawning time between now and being with Joe. She wants to keep Pia happy, keep her smiling. Wants Joe to like what he sees.

At the harbour, Marie is almost first off the bus (would have been first if not for a man's oversized suitcase and the fact she is carrying a baby in her arms). Trying not to run across the stones. Seeing the fishing nets glinting silver. Eyes scanning the names of the boats and the faces of the men all around.

Seeing Joe's boat: *Green Tara*.

Clattering down the gangplank in high white heels.

Marie waves at one of Joe's crewmen, but he either does not see or does not recognise her.

Pete – she calls excitedly – I'm here to see Joe.

He's in his cabin, says Pete. And then slowly: Marie, is that you?

Of course it's me. Thinking: do I look too fat to go in there? Trying to read Pete's eyes. His thin brown face that time has done nothing to.

Marie hesitates outside Joe's door, smoothing her hair into place, rearranging Pia. Sending up a small, silent prayer:

Dear God, make him want to be with us. Make him take us away with him, away from everything here.

Joe is lying on his back on his bed, eyes closed, one arm drawn tight across them.

The light, he says, not moving a muscle, the light makes the pain worse.

Then: is that you Marie?

She says, yes, walking to stand beside him.

Put your hand on my head, will you?

Marie silently shifts Pia on to her hip, places her fingers on Joe's head.

Is that better?

Move your fingers in circles, he says, still not looking at her. A little bit slower, over to the left. Yes, he says, yes that's it.

They stay like that for a while: Joe with his eyes closed on the bed, Marie standing over him with her baby resting on her hip and her fingers tracing Joe's hairline. She hears the gulls calling outside the window. In the next cabin, the sound of banging as Joe's neighbour moves his furniture about.

Not much to do here, Joe says grimly, from morning to evening. Sometimes it helps to rearrange your cabin. Or see a pretty, friendly face.

He sits up now and slowly moves his arm away from his eyes. Opens them gingerly. Shuts them tight again immediately.

Marie is not sure if he had a chance to see her, her or Pia, but he is keeping his eyes squeezed shut now and the waiting is an agony so she says:

I have something to show you.

Joe opens one eye, and then the other. Looking straight at Pia and at the top of Marie's leg.

Marie squats until her eyes are level with his, puts the baby on to the bed.

Her name is Pia. Don't you think she's a wonder?

A wonder, yes, he says, she makes me wonder why have you brought her here and – looking suddenly at Marie's face, seeing the swollen roundness of her, the dimples in her arms – what has happened to you?

Blushing and feeling like a whale in her grey coat, Marie says: post-baby weight.

I see, he says, the baby is yours.

Pia starts to cry, wrinkling up her face and making fists and Joe's palms start to feel itchy, unaccountably, rubbing them vigorously up and down his legs, liking the feel of the rough cotton scratching at them. Wanting to blink the whole scene away. This young girl swollen almost to non-recognition and the baby on his bed with a ridiculous bow in her hair.

I have a hangover.

Joe is speaking the words under his breath. Pia has stopped crying but still Marie cannot hear him, so she asks him to say it again.

I have a hangover.

I guessed that.

It hurts to keep my eyes open.

And he collapses back on to the bed and puts both arms this time over his eyes.

In the silence, Marie fidgets with Pia, frothing out her dress and picking stray hairs off her tights. The room is very still. Not much movement in the sea today. The room is hot and smells of damp wood and diesel. A pile of clothes crumpled in a corner.

Marie picks them up and begins to fold them. I'll clean these for you, she says, if you like.

He says: I think you'd better leave – my headache, it's making me feel nauseous.

She says: I can return them to you in a few days. Clean and pressed. I know how you like clean clothes.

No, leave them.

Sitting up now and his head is banging.

I made a mistake, he says, asking you to come. It was the spur of the moment, he says, I'm sorry.

Sorry?

I'll call you again, in a few days, when I'm feeling better.

You won't.

I will, he says, I promise. I'm just not up to – he folds his arms over his eyes again – entertaining. Then wearily: I'm not good with children. They drive me— She can barely hear him now, just the sound of him mumbling. She thinks she hears him correctly. They drive me insane.

There is a dark mark by Pia's nose that Marie picks at with a painted nail. Standing at the bus stop on the harbour, buffeted by the salt wind.

Marie thinks of Sam: his blue eyes, his slim hands, the way he holds Pia against him as if she is precious, very precious. Marie feels his shape alongside hers in the bed; familiar now with the curves and crooks of his body because he moulds himself into her in the night. Fits himself around her so that she wakes, so boxed in by him it takes moments to be sure whose leg is whose, whose heavy crushing arm.

She will get on the bus, when it comes, go home, cook Sam something to eat. She will bathe Pia, put her to bed and sit in front of the gas fire with Sam.

Marie pays her money to the conductor, holding the coins out to him but staring into space.

Pretty baby, he says.

He smiles at Pia and then looks at Marie.

Pretty mother too.

And just for a moment Marie feels light. Not fat, in this moment, not ugly, her whole life ripped apart.

When the bus reaches her stop, the doors open and Marie stays seated. Watches the old woman get off the bus, leaning heavily on a stick. Then the doors close with a hiss and the bus is off.

Off.

Marie looking out of the window, leaving behind familiar shops and streets and houses, feels them falling away. Like her life with Sam, dropping away behind her, like clothing thrown out of the window, first her heavy grey coat, her scarf, her shoes, her red and black plastic bag.

It is dark when the bus reaches the depot. Just Marie, Pia and the conductor on the bus now.

End of the line, the conductor says, walking to the back of the bus where they are seated.

I know, Marie says.

She starts to gather her things together, slips her feet back into her shoes, feels them pinch her toes.

Got far to go? he asks.

I'm not sure.

Not sure?

No, she says. She feels the beginning of tears. It has taken all she has to get her to this point and now—

The conductor looks at the girl slumping on the seat in front of him, looks at her coat and sparkly dress, the baby sleeping on her lap.

He says: can I invite you for a cup of tea? and Marie looks up at him gratefully.

Yes, she says, thank you.

Marie follows the conductor off the bus and into the brightly lit staff canteen. She sits at a long table with her daughter. The conductor brings her a saucer of custard creams and bourbons that are broken at the corners. A cheese sandwich for himself.

They eat in silence, Marie conscious only of the sweet taste of the biscuits, the sensation of them dissolving in her mouth. The quiet relief that there is another one to reach out for, and then another and another.

When they have finished eating, they all walk out on to the

forecourt of the depot. Floodlit black tarmac, the clatter of diesels dying down.

Where now then? the conductor asks, passing Marie's bag back to her. He ruffles Pia's hair.

Marie shrugs.

No idea at all?

No, Marie says, no idea at all, and something about her own voice (the way it quivers as she says, *at all*, the frightened way she sounds) makes her start to cry, standing on the pavement under a street light.

Pia's eyes are heavy, her eyelids are closing. The bow in her hair is crumpled into a knot.

The conductor says: my bedsit is only a five minute walk away, and the three of them trudge through the streets in silence, the conductor carrying Marie's bag.

The conductor's room is cramped, walkways crammed between boxes and chairs. Newspapers, pictures and china ornaments dangling on edges and leaning against walls. A chipped enamel cooker in the corner. A table spread with all manner of broken things. Marie fingers a bronze kettle, a dismantled toaster, the oily insides of a still-ticking clock.

Not much room, he says, even for me. But I manage.

Feeling suddenly shy now. Seeing his room through a stranger's eyes.

Just for one night, he says. You will have to leave in the morning.

Thank you, Marie says, trying to find a space to put Pia down.

The conductor makes a bed on his pale orange carpet. A few dusty cushions, a blanket patched with burn marks, a sheet decorated with pictures of trains.

He stirs a pan of hot chocolate, his tiny body hunched over the cooker.

The alarm will go off at six, he says. I have to be away by six thirty.

He passes Marie a steaming mug.

Help yourself to whatever food there is.

Thank you.

If you want you can use the telephone, he says, make plans for wherever you need to go.

When he turns out the light, she can hear the conductor undressing in the darkness. Marie remains bundled in her coat, one arm around her daughter's waist.

All the next day, Marie stays lying on the conductor's floor. When Pia wakes, Marie feeds and strokes her. They are both very quiet. As if in the silence, they can somehow disappear.

They are still there when the conductor gets home from work. He unwraps a greasy packet of fish and chips on to the kitchen table.

Only bought enough for one, he says dividing up the portion on to mismatched plates.

He finds a few toffees in a jar, half a bar of chocolate and a bottle of lemonade, gulping from the bottle, wiping the top with his sleeve and then passing it to Marie.

She polishes the food off in minutes. It barely hits the sides of her belly.

You want to stay another night?

Yes, she says. And then: I'm sorry. The baby's father, she says and then falters. He doesn't want us. And I married another man and I don't love him.

She looks at the conductor's face and he is still looking at her.

It's such a mess. I've made such a mess of my life.

Marie says: I saw my lover's wife in a photograph. She looked like she had everything she could possibly want.

Life is not about want, says the conductor. No one has everything.

No, Marie agrees. But some people definitely have more.

Feeling so hungry now, she has to ask him: do you have anything else to eat?

He finds a packet of crisps and a small bag of raisins.

Not used to having people around, he says. Not the way that I have mapped out my life. And besides, he says, there's not enough room and we don't know each other and—

It's all right, Marie says. It's not your problem. It doesn't matter.

She says she is tired and he turns out the light.

That night in his sleep, there are snakes around the conduc-, tor's ankles. Sees them crawling all over the girl on his floor and her baby. Wakes up kicking them off, saying: all right you can stay, we'll find a way round it. Not sure how, but I've made up my mind.

There is no reply so the conductor looks across the floor to where Marie and Pia were sleeping. Finds only a pile of folded bedding and thank you scribbled on an envelope.

home

Sam tells the police officer: we have only been married a year.

Red-eyed, pacing the room.

It's been over twenty-four hours, he says, since I have seen them. Marie my wife, he explains, and Pia, our child.

Did you have an argument? the police officer asks.

No.

But you have no idea where she has gone?

No, says Sam.

What about a friend's house?

And although he spoke to her friend Anna only an hour before, getting on the telephone again, in front of the policeman, dialling Anna's number, asking the same words in the same sequence: have you heard from Marie?

No, says Anna. She's still not home?

No.

Don't worry. She'll be back.

And Anna sounds so sure, Sam asks her: how can you be certain?

Certain?

Anna is not certain about anything – her own husband, Steve, snoring softly now on the sofa, one hand still clasped round a wineglass.

Wondering: would Steve miss me? Would he sound so empty, so on the edge of hysteria?

She's lucky to have you.

Saying the words although they have not fully formed in her head and so they surprise her.

Thank you, says Sam quietly. But it's Pia that I miss.

The thought that he has lost Pia makes him feel like punching the walls and, at the same time, curling up in a small ball on the floor beside them.

And where is Marie? No closer to knowing her than the night he first met her and she made him take her home.

She did not make him, no. Even now, he remembers the excitement he felt at having a girl in his bedroom. The taste of dark rum and her kisses. He has no one to blame but himself.

Has she done this before?

Done what?

Sam looks at the police officer's mean little mouth, a yellow moustache sitting on it like the tail of a reptile.

Disappeared overnight.

We've only been married a year.

Has she been distressed? asks the officer. Has anything been troubling her?

Maybe she has been abducted, says Sam. Have you thought about that?

In cases such as this—

Such as what?

The police officer spits the word out – domestics – shiny as a marble. We usually give it a day or so.

And then?

The wife usually comes back.

Moments later, there she is, standing in the doorway, hair flat against her head. And Pia, his darling Pia, asleep in her arms. Sam rushes towards Marie, pulls the baby out of her arms as if she is a parcel, thinks Marie: something to be pulled away and grabbed.

And the police officer says: see, I told you. The first years of marriage are the worst.

The police officer is smiling now, exhibiting a row of perfect, even teeth.

My wife and I thought we would never survive it. It was the shock – he smiles knowingly at them – getting to know someone new. And compromise – he is standing at the door now but reluctant, still, to go – marriage is all about compromise. Once you accept that, he claps his hands together and the buttons on his sleeves begin to quiver. You're home and dry, he says.

Home and dry.

Those three words linger in Marie's head long after the police officer has left and Sam has closed the door behind him. Linger long after the silence that sits inside the room blocking the air and the light. Long after Sam tells her: I hate you—

I hate you.

Now Marie has a word for the feeling that sits between

them. She had not been sure that was what it was, but now she knows.

She's not your baby.

Marie says the words for the taste of them, for the look she sees sweep across Sam's features, for the sweet, sharp heat in her belly and the flush rising to her face.

At once the room is still, like a moment freeze-framed in a photograph.

Wondering if, maybe, he will drop her: the child he is holding on to like a possession in a storm.

She is not yours.

The words are less sharp the second time around, but still they hurt him. And although he has heard them inside his head every day for over a year, in this moment he does not believe them. They cannot be true.

He says: you want to hurt me.

Yes, she says. I want to hurt you.

She walks towards him until her toes are almost touching his.

And, she says, it is also true.

Sam has never hit a woman. Never thought a woman could deserve—

Drawing back his arm, feeling the soft flesh of Marie's face crumple, turning inside out underneath his fist and a smarting at his knuckles.

Sam would hit her again but he knows if he does he won't be able to stop.

Marie talks less and less. Is quiet even when she is out with Anna. Silently spooning trifle into her mouth.

Where did you go?

Marie says: I'm sorry, I can't tell you.

Do you plan to stay now, with Sam and Pia?

Marie nods but her eyes do not leave her plate.

Cakes and biscuits hidden all over the house. The food-stashes give Marie a sense of almost well-being. It is the knowledge of their existence that enables her to get on with her life. Hoover the floor then have a handful of digestive biscuits. Clean out the bath, a packet of crisps and half a Mars Bar – saving the other half until she has lifted all the towels from the bathroom floor and picked Sam's hairs out of the soap dish. Sitting on the toilet seat and biting into the half-eaten Mars with a sigh.

But then Pia starts to scream and it is hard to concentrate on the taste in her mouth, the textures. On and on the child is screaming, as if Marie has nothing better to do.

Nothing better to do than to go in there and pander to her. She gets everything she wants (food, baths, attention, clothes). Why can't she let Marie have a few moments for herself?

All right, she yells. All right, I'm coming.

Stamping down the hallway to the room where the baby cries.

For goodness' sake.

Picking her up and holding her against her shoulder.

Stop that crying.

Banging her on the back three times, four.

Come on, stop it.

The baby is screaming into her ear. And Marie has so much to do today – all she's been able to think about since she got up this morning is when she can get back to bed, she could quite happily never leave her bedroom, never do another thing for another person, never pick up another pan, never wash another sock. Whatever the baby is needing she simply does not have it. *She does not have it.*

Feels herself shaking again, shaking and shaking the screaming baby. When the telephone rings it seems to call her back from a faraway place. She walks across the room to pick up the telephone.

Yes Sam, Pia's fine, Marie says. We have both been asleep.

another home

At work, Sam keeps his head down, but he has ideas. Big ideas. Sam wants to make money, wants to be successful, wants his father to feel – sorry. Yes, sorry, that he did not believe in him. Just to hear the old man say it: well done. It shouldn't mean so much, but it does.

Sam has a new car. He polishes it until he can see his face in it, his and Pia's and Marie's. Dressed up in their best new clothes.

Lunch in a hotel.

Sam likes the way the words sound when he says them.

Come on, he says, it will be a treat.

Combing tonic through his hair.

They pull out on to the road and the sun is shining. How green the little squares of lawn and the leaves in the trees.

Sam got a pay rise on Friday, together with a promotion.

Like the way you work, his manager said. Got a bright future ahead of you.

Sam feels tall sitting in the front seat of his shiny blue car. Song words tripping round in his head: if I had a hammer . . . hammer in the morning . . . evening . . . all over this land.

Marie sits with her bag resting on her knees. Occasionally

looking over her shoulder at Pia. Pia smiling in the back seat of her father's brand new car.

Sam rolls film tracks in his head, lingering on favourite scenes: Sam and another woman on the top of a mountain surrounded by snow, Sam and another woman with his parents in a garden, Sam and another woman and Pia in a big wooden house.

But you can't do that with life, he thinks, chop it all up and put the pieces back together in a different order.

You reach a point – his father told him the day he sent him to college – where you realise you are no longer a boy. You have a grown-up life you would not necessarily have chosen, but it is your grown-up life and you have to live it to the end.

Living it to the end, did the old man regret a lot of things? Would he regret turning his back on Sam and Pia?

In a circle, Sam's thoughts, always returning to the old man. As if his life is incomplete without him. As if he is the pivot on which the whole thing turns.

And just as suddenly as Sam feels the lightness in his ribcage, the feeling he is certain other people would call happiness, something like a grey cloud is descending and he doesn't feel like lunch in the hotel, doesn't feel much like anything at all.

Sun disappearing now behind a cloud and the streets look grey again, grey and littered and cold.

Driving past the restaurant and Marie says: where are we going?

Driving past the park, the old school and the swimming pool. Sam finds himself following a route he used to take as a teenager, along the railway track then a sharp left and a right. New zebra crossing, a new grocer's shop on the corner called: Vilatella's.

When Sam comes to a halt it is outside his parents' house. He sits in silence for a while, looking at the glass panels in the front door. The apple tree in the garden and a mass of buttercups all around.

Are you going to go in? Marie asks him.

I haven't decided.

Then why are we here?

I don't know, he says. I don't know.

Getting out of the car to get away from Marie as much as to walk across the road and stand for a moment at the whitewashed gate.

He sees the curtain ripple. A shadow behind the net. Then a face at the window.

It seems an eternity to Sam – standing on the pavement outside the home of his childhood – then he hears the clatter of the latch and his mother is standing at the front door.

Stepping into the garden.

Sam, she says.

Standing in the shadow of the apple tree which spreads

out its branches as if to echo the old woman hunching in on herself.

Sam's mother says: I am so sorry. Not my fault, she says. You know your father—

I know, says Sam, not wanting to hear it. I know.

It's not as if I haven't thought of you, as if I haven't wanted—

Speaking to her now with a gate between them and an expanse of garden. What to tell her, across the distance?

Asking: is the old man at home?

No, not for another hour.

Feeling relief and a deep stabbing pain.

Would you like to see your grandchild?

Sam's mother steps forward, moving across the grass as if each step hurts her.

Are you all right?

Yes, she says.

She smiles a smile like a reed skimming water.

Marie is getting out of the car, standing in the middle of the road, holding their baby.

Is that her?

Sam's mother starts moving towards Marie. My granddaughter – is that her?

Marie holds out her free hand and Sam's mother holds on to it.

This is Pia.

Passing her to her, and as their two heads touch Sam has to look away.

Look away from his mother, her grey shape almost melting with the heat and the newness and the fear that the old man will soon be back.

Sam feels, for a moment, that he is the centre of a family, the middle of three generations and that life is a continuous line. A continuous line flowing from one person into the next so that nothing is for nothing and everything makes sense.

Ought to go inside – it is his mother speaking – before it gets cold.

It's not cold, Sam says.

But he sees his mother shivering.

You can't depend, she says, on these warm bright days. They change so quickly.

She starts to move towards the house.

You want to go in? Marie asks Sam.

Not sure if they are invited. But seeing his mother's shape disappearing inside the door, Sam knows he is not ready to leave.

Sam and Marie walk across the lawn, crushing daisies. Sam remembers his father loves daisies. Daisies and buttercups. He called them nature's own. Stooping in the long grass to smell and touch but never to pick them. He treated them with a wonder he reserved only for them.

Seated with the old woman now round the table. Hearing the ticking again of the mantelpiece clock – unmoved. Unmoved too the china figurine of a clown playing a lute, and an old woman made out of clay bending in the shade of some trees. Dust free beside the clock on the mantel. Same cushion covers, same plates and cups for tea.

Not sure what to ask her now that he's here and it's all so familiar. Like nothing has happened since Sam was last at this table, not to this house or its inhabitants, or to him. Like it was all a dream – going away to study, the girl in the library, Marie and Pia, his promotion, his new car.

And besides it was always the old man he imagined revisiting. Stacks of things he had to say to him.

But her? This shadow of a woman? What to say except:

It's good to see you.

And: it all looks the same, he says, in here, nothing has altered.

I've altered, says his mother but so quietly he cannot be sure that he heard her.

Did you say something?

Going now, she says, to boil the water. (Sounds like alter, he thinks, also like ought to. She has not changed, thinks Sam, only disappeared a little more.)

How do you stand it?

Sam is suddenly standing up and banging his fist on the table. So much energy now that he is inside of these walls and they want to crush him again. This tiny, motionless room.

He has to remind himself: I have been away from here, I have seen other things, I am not a boy now. It is the thought of his father coming back. The remnants of the feeling he leaves lying around.

Stand what?

His mother walking back into the lounge with the tea tray.

Not having your own life.

What are you talking about?

Being dominated by him.

His mother stands in front of him; her hair is wispy as candy floss and she is stroking a few strands off of her face.

Sugar, she says at last. I knew there was something I had forgotten.

And she walks away from him and back into the kitchen.

Marie and Sam reach out for triangles of sandwich and sip tea. Sam's mother looks at her watch. She cannot sit still for more than a few minutes, walking to the window, peering outside.

They are waiting – though none of them will say it – for the old man to get back, for the way he will make everything change. Sam hears his heart beating inside of his new shirt, hears the ticking of the clock, the tinkle sound of Marie's bangle as it taps against her plate. He has imagined this meeting so many times.

Let me win, thinks Sam.

Though he is not sure what winning would mean.

The door slams and at the same moment, Sam's father calls for his wife:

Selina.

Jumping up so fast she knocks her cup to the floor. Bending down with her tissue to mop up the tea.

Calling for her again although it is only seconds since the last time.

Selina. Where are you?

In the lounge, she says. We have visitors—

And now he is inside of the room. Seeing Sam, seeing Marie. And the shape bundled in white on his armchair. Speechless for a moment, inside his own house, something he has forbidden.

What is the meaning—?

Sam feels tiny in his chair while his father is the size of his house.

They were just passing – Sam's mother is on her feet now – they have only been here a few minutes.

Sam wants to get out of his chair, stand in front of his father, stand so at least his eyes may be level with his. Marie is looking at him. He knows she is thinking he is a coward. He knows his mother has only moments until she—

I'm sorry, she says.

I will deal with you, Sam's father says, later.

Turning to Sam (why can't he get out of his chair, why

won't his legs let him? Sinking further into his shirt and the carpet feels like the sea).

Why are you here?

Why am I here? The sentence is running around inside Sam's head like a caged animal – a caged animal that does not know what to do with its new-found freedom so it keeps on banging into the same four walls.

To show you this – Marie holds Pia out to Sam's father. Sam thought you might like to see her: Pia, your grand-child.

Marie speaking for him and to Sam it feels like betrayal.

My daughter, says Sam, staggering to his feet and now he is standing the room feels very different. There is grey in his father's hair. Standing there rooted but swaying from side to side with his hand against his mouth.

I am a father now, says Sam. This is my family, he says. I wanted—

Marie sits down. Sam's father is not speaking and the room is very still.

I have just had a promotion.

The words come out weakly. He feels like a boy holding out his report card.

Aren't you proud of me? – watching his father leave the room, biting down the words he will never, must never speak.

Sitting there in his absence, his huge, aching absence, Sam

pushes his fists into his legs to stop himself running after the old man. Wanting to shake him, to hear those old bones rattle, to make him let go of the hold that he has.

His mother is sniffling into a handkerchief. The bones of her shoulders spike her dress like pyramids. Mottled grey legs although the late sun still shines.

You shouldn't have come.

Sam's mother does not look at him.

You've made it all worse, she says. Much, much worse.

Outside in the car, Marie fiddles with the buttons on the radio while Sam walks round the car.

Not wanting to drive straight home, so driving them all to the hotel.

Bundling Marie through the front door although she says: I am tired.

I want to celebrate, he says.

Celebrate what?

That I'm better than he is.

Better than your father?

Sam, ordering smoked salmon and avocado soup.

The old man has never eaten like this, he says, will never eat smoked salmon off a silver fork.

The most expensive fish, he orders, wine and every type of vegetable: asparagus, artichokes, long green beans.

What would you like for dessert?

Marie hovers over the menu – how to decide?

A portion of everything, says Sam feeling magnificently reckless. My wife wants to taste everything.

Chocolates, sorbets, fruits in caramelised pastry cases, marzipan, thin mints and rivers of cream. They pile the plates around Marie until she feels like a princess. Decorously sampling a mouthful of pistachio, leaning across a platter of pineapple with a long-handled spoon.

Sam watches Marie and he feels an anger rising. He wants her to feel happy but it is all her fault. He asks for the bill and as he pays for the desserts, Sam hates her. Hates her as he leads her out to the car. Hates her the whole silent journey home.

paper

So when, later that night, Marie says: I'm pregnant again, Sam asks: whose baby?

Whose baby? – Marie is startled by the suggestion.

You heard me, Sam says, who is the father?

It's you of course.

Sam says sarcastically: of course.

What are you talking about?

I'm talking about Pia, Sam says, how can I believe you have been faithful? Why should I believe there is no one else?

Because there isn't, says Marie. Because I'm telling you the truth. Because I thought you would be happy to be a father again.

Do you want me to get rid of it – get rid of the baby? she asks.

His baby. Get rid of his baby?

This one must be his.

Who else would look twice, he thinks, at Marie? Backside the size of a house.

Sam has only had sex with her twice in the last four months – and both times he was drunk and she was very passive.

You just lie there, doing nothing – he told her. But she had evidently been doing something.

A child of his own.

But in a marriage already curling at the edges like a loaf of stale bread.

A brother or sister, he thinks, for Pia.

I don't know what I want, he says.

And so the baby grows by default. Neither of them taking the decision to kill it. Neither of them saying: I want this child.

Until one day Marie says: I am seven months pregnant.

And Sam finds himself saying: I'm glad.

Glad?

Yes, says Sam.

Sam buys a mobile of little paper ships dangling on fishing wire. If the child is a boy, he thinks, I will give it to him. A secret present – in the drawer of his desk – for his now hoped-for son.

The baby is not due for three weeks but it is hammering and hammering on the inside of her body so that Marie feels faint sitting there in the garden, in the shade of the lilac tree, calls out for Sam and then for Anna, inside together in the kitchen.

Quick, she says, come quickly.

Is it time?

Yes, Marie says, it's time.

No time to call the doctor, screaming now into the July

sunshine, because she cannot take the pain and there is no one to take it away.

Luke is fat and red and screaming, his whole body screwed up like a fist. And Sam standing over her now with green eyes, green green eyes saying: it's going to be all right, all right now and Marie wants, so wants to believe him, clinging on to his hand as she is lifted into the ambulance.

They let Pia ride up at the front and one of the ambulance men squeezes her knee and calls her:
Princess.
Princess. Makes Pia think of the girls in her story books, girls who end up with castles, princes, gold and jewels – however they start out. No matter how low.
Princess Pia. Like he knows. The games she plays when she is on her own and she can pretend any life that she wants. She takes her father with her sometimes. Into a land where her mother does not exist. That is the main thing. Every time. Always. To pretend there is no Marie.

I hate my mother, Pia once told a school friend.
The school friend did not believe her. No one hates their mother, she said, not truly. Not for long.
So Pia found an imaginary friend – she discovered a name for her when she saw a similar girl peering out at her from the pages of a story book – lady-in-waiting. They sit up late at night

telling each other stories. When Marie's mother looks in to check up on them, they compete to see who can remain the most quiet.

The other girls in the playground seem bigger. To Pia. Longer arms and legs. Stronger, wider too. They take up a lot of space – skipping ropes and plastic bags filled with packets of sweets and silver-wrapped biscuits. She does not know what to do to join in. An invisible game, with invisible rules. The lady-in-waiting likes to walk in the back field, so Pia joins her in the break times, wandering round and around.

They like her stories, the teachers say, they like her poems. Pinning them up on the walls with coloured stars.

When her mother finds out, she buys Pia a cake with icing on it and sits with her at the table. Marie looks happy, Pia thinks, in that moment. Shiny blue eyes.

But it does not last.

So soon, it seems, Pia does something again to make her mother angry. Not turning off the television quick enough, not hearing her name the moment her mother calls her and—

Marie is tired and it has been three nights since Sam has been home. Anna was going to come over this afternoon but her son has a cold and she stayed at home with him and sometimes it seems there is not another adult in the entire universe, just babies and all their baby things – and what do you get for it, what do you get?

Calling: Pia.

Makes her feel good to think of her daughter's work on the wall in the school corridor and the classroom. Not done everything wrong after all. Pia said they want her to play a princess in the school play. Not done everything wrong, but the house is a mess and she feels so tired—

Calling Pia again.

Why don't you come when I call you?

Pia running into the kitchen now.

I'm sorry.

Sorry? Don't you think I have enough to do? says Marie. Without running around after you and trying to get your attention? When I call what are you supposed to do?

Come straight away.

That's right. How many times do I have to tell you? When will you learn Pia? When will you start behaving yourself?

Saying the same words again: I am sorry.

And if you don't come when you're called, says Marie, then what?

Pia's bottom lip begins to feel heavy, there are tears smarting her eyes.

Standing still for the flat hand sting that feels like a bite and a grazing.

You're a bad girl. You ruin everything. Everything, Marie says.

Marie is always sorry. Very sorry. She buys Pia bags of sweets and, once, a doll with a button on her stomach to make her hair grow.

There now. Are you feeling better?

Anna says: you spoil her.

But sometimes Anna does not like the look she sees in Pia's eyes. Sometimes the child is so quiet it makes her feel uncomfortable.

Squatting down to bring her eyes level with Pia's

Is there something wrong?

Shaking her head from side to side and just standing there. Not running up and down like the other kids. She never looks really happy. Never looks like a child, Anna thinks.

Once Anna saw Marie hitting Pia and it was not one time or two – she was beating her about the arms and face and it was over and over.

What are you doing?

In the end Anna had to intervene, there was only so long she could stand there and watch.

Stop it Marie. She had to shout at her. It's not right. Come on. Stop it.

Pulling her off. Thinking: Marie is out of control. But don't we all feel like that – deranged, unhinged – once in a while? Giving Pia a marshmallow square and wanting to cuddle her, but she seemed entirely made of ice.

Anna thought things would get better once the little boy was born. But Marie does not warm to him. Although she never hits him. Pia always seems to get in the way.

There is a bond between Pia and Luke. Of that Anna is certain. Their eyes seek each other's out in any room. Never too far apart. She'd swear they talk without either of them speaking. Leaving the room at the same moment without a sign or a mention. Both suddenly looking up at the same thing, reaching for the same toy, making the same shape with their hands.

Extraordinary children, thinks Anna, glad they are not hers. Glad her son is normal. Always playing with the other kids on the street. Not clinging to his sister, like Luke.

Tonight when Sam collects Marie and the children from Anna's house and Marie is upstairs in the bathroom, Sam kisses her. Kisses Anna as she is putting a spoonful of coffee into a mug for him and thinking: he smells nice.

What do you think you are doing?

Kissing you.

Sam is smiling.

What for?

And hearing her own voice she feels such an idiot. Standing there in an old jumper – she wishes she had thought to comb her hair, slippers scuffed around the edges and all under his big green eyes.

What do you think I did it for?

Then Marie is back in the room and so are the children and everything is noisy and bustling and she doesn't catch his gaze again although she retains it. Retains it behind her eyelids and replays it that night while her husband Steve snores in his sleep.

A woman like Marie how could she ever be enough, thinks Anna, for a man like Sam? Anna is fond of her of course, they have a lot in common – well mainly it is the children – but she is a good sort, got a good heart, doesn't mean to do wrong but she's like a little girl.

A little girl, thinks Anna, not much brightness to Marie at all.

And then there is Sam, polished up and professional. He knows things. You only have to look at him to see that. All those numbers and symbols clanging around in his head, makes a woman feel quite breathless. Feeling breathless now thinking about him in the early morning.

Not sure what she is contemplating, having always been faithful (in body if not inside her head) – getting stirred by other women's husbands all the time, if she is honest, not content with Steve, but then who could be? No more affection in him than in a toaster; lot less heat. She finds herself smiling. Smiling as she thinks of Sam again.

Remembering when Marie went missing it was Pia, Sam told her, it was Pia that he missed. Marie is lucky to have him. If she does not realise it she is an idiot. An idiot who deserves—

Anna gets up and goes to the bathroom to get a glass of water.

An idiot who deserves – a better friend than Anna, Anna reminds herself.

But feeling the creeping heat again as she slips under the duvet, thinking: there is no fault in fantasising. No – seeing Sam's face again and deciding there is no harm in fantasising at all.

Anna goes up on the train to meet Sam at his office because he says, I think there are things we need to talk about, don't you?

Talk about, yes, she says but as the train shudders forward she is not thinking about talking to Sam. Not constructing sentences and restaurant scenes in her head. Impossible to stop the flow of thoughts about his – textures, the way he feels, thinks Anna.

After eight years of touching a man like stone.

Sam's office: a brown room, battered leather swivel chair and so many papers everywhere, covering every surface. She can barely read the words that are written on them let alone make them make sense.

A clever man, she thinks, and the pictures begin again.

An Italian restaurant, red and white and green, the waiters almost bowing as they walk inside. They know Sam, he has a favourite table. Pulling Anna's chair out for her beside a small barred window and then she is sitting opposite Sam, only a small square of table between – and a salt cellar, a bread bowl, two glasses, two plates, a red paper cloth—

Lots to talk about, he'd said and she'd agreed, but now it seems there is nothing. Eating their food in silence, swirling spaghetti strings and he says:

What time do you have to get back?

Wiping the corners of his mouth with a serviette. Looking at his watch.

It is only half past twelve and he is buttoning her into her coat and all the time he is looking away.

He says he will walk her to the station on his way back to the office—

No problem, he says, really no problem—

But walking one or two steps in front of her.

Hearing the clicking of their heels on the pavement, Anna thinks: how did it go so wrong? It had all the ingredients, she thinks, but falling so flat.

Is it Marie? she wants to ask him. Is it because of a sense of guilt? She could understand. Would understand. Would not then need to go home feeling like a—

Failure, she thinks. Other women manage it all the time. Is it something about me?

Asking: is it something about me? because they are only seconds from the station—

Something about you?

Yes.

What do you mean?

Lunch, she says, stopping dead in the street and a man with a briefcase collides with her, trying to get past.

Sam has stopped too, turning to face her on the pavement.

Was it so awful? she says and, for a moment, Sam sees in her what he saw when he asked her to lunch

Not so awful, he says and there is a crookedness to his mouth when he smiles.

Want a coffee in my office?

Yes, she says, relieved.

But, following him, still walking a pace or two behind.

He fills the kettle from the tap. She hears it dripping as he plugs the kettle in at the wall and says: all mod cons

Yes, she says, I can see that.

A packet of digestive biscuits, milk in the fridge alongside test tubes and bottles of turquoise and thick green liquids.

A Sales Rep's samples, he says as she crouches in front of the fridge door with him.

Are they poisonous?

No, he says, not really.

What does 'not really' mean?

It's a question of amount, he says. Take too much of anything and it will make you feel ill.

She wants to dip her fingers into the different test tubes, touch and taste the chemical liquids.

It is another world, she says.

He says: I get excited by answers.

By knowing things, she says, you are less likely to be caught out

Going back on the train. The end of a day I have thought and dreamed of – and I cannot say the air crackled between us, Anna thinks, cannot say that it was inevitable, unstoppable, special even, I cannot say that, but—

When he reached for me, turning away from the fridge and his knee knocked against mine, I thought: why not?

The thick taste of his tongue, not what I had imagined – such a precise, edged man I expected a line and an accuracy to his movements. But he was sloppy, urgent. Leaning me backwards over his desk on to all those papers – a silver pot stacked with pens, I pushed it to the floor just to hear the noise.

Brown cork tiles on the walls and pinned to one of them a silver-grey butterfly, looked like it was resting there on the wall until you looked closely, saw the tiny pins in its wings.

He didn't kiss me again, did not take off my dress, did not tell me that he loved me but the feel of him inside of me, a stranger. It made me feel unlike myself, like someone exotic, unusual. I exploded with him, though the feeling caught me out and the noise I was making, biting down on the sleeve of his coat.

He left me instantly, turning back to the fridge. I saw that he was shaking. We drank our coffee in silence. It was still surprisingly hot.

I felt tingly. Sweat on my back underneath my dress. I rearranged my clothes in silence. I could go home now feeling – feeling – I've done it. Yes, she thinks, simple as that. I have done it.

I applied my lipstick while he looked at me. Walked out on to an unfamiliar street.

And I walked differently, I am sure of it. Hugging my secret, like a present, close to me. I was not the woman that people saw. I am not now.

Anna telephones Marie from the station, because she is her friend, because she has to have someone who knows:

I made love this afternoon, she breathes into the telephone, to a strange man, in his office.

Who was he? It is Marie's first question.

No one you know. Anna says: don't you want to know about it?

Yes, of course.

Then why all the questions?

It's been – Marie says – a bad day.

Anna can hear Pia crying in the background.

I've not seen Sam for two days.

Brushing her teeth and looking at her face in the mirror, Anna thinks: it can be as if things have not happened. In the space of a few hours – the hours between talking to Marie on the telephone and coming home, here, to her house and her husband – the afternoon has been erased. What does she have to prove it happened? That she felt the way she did?

Running to her bag, rummaging through it. Finding the train ticket (dated, hole-punched by the conductor) and the wrapper from a packet of chewing gum – chewing gum that she bought as she stood on the station platform thinking about going to meet Sam, remembering that.

Thinking: I should write it all down, somewhere, make notes. Because soon there will be nothing left.

Finding a biro at the bottom of her bag – Caledonian Airways, one of Steve's, from his travels – scribbling:

Sam, Tuesday 24th June, brown office, pot of pencils, felt unlike me.

rain

At first Marie notices only that Anna is visiting more, telephoning more, dropping round late at night.

And always wearing lipstick.

She is very quiet with Sam at first. The pair of them silent in each other's company. Marie talking and talking to fill up the space.

One night Marie and Sam have been fighting and when the knock comes at the door, Sam seems pleased – no delighted – to see Anna. Showing her a book he has been reading.

Just to annoy me, thinks Marie, to make me feel that I am a fool.

But then one night when Marie says: I am going to bed,

Anna does not leave – does not leave immediately as she usually does, but says:

I think I'll stay for one more drink, a night cap.

And it does not feel like such a game then. Walking up the stairs there is lead in Marie's legs. She wants to go back down and grab hold of Anna, grab hold of her by the sleeve of her new dress and turf her on to the street.

It's not that Marie wants Sam for herself. Not really. It's just that it's an –

Affront—

The word comes suddenly to Marie and hits the perfect note – for how she is feeling, for what is being done to her.

So she goes back down the stairs and marches into the lounge where they are sitting.

I think you'd better go – glaring now at Anna. It is late and Steve will be concerned.

Yes, says Anna, I'm sure you're right.

If Sam had not walked Anna to the door, Marie might be feeling better now – now that she has marked out her territory and drawn battle lines. But although Anna has gone and Sam is lying there beside Marie and she is listening to his breathing – still she feels her world is sliding.

Marie broaches the subject the next morning, over tea and marmalade on toast.

Anna seems to be coming over a lot.

Looking up from his toast, Sam says: does she?

Yes and she seems to like talking to you.

Yes.

And you? Marie says.

Me?

Do you like talking to her?

Marie is losing her temper. Talking to Sam is like talking to the wardrobe. All that stuff folded away inside. She wants an answer out of him. An answer or a reaction. So bloody stiff and quiet, he is.

So bloody Sam.

What?

Are you having an affair?

An affair? Sam says. Don't be ridiculous.

Because they are not. Not then.

But after Marie suggests it, it becomes a possibility.

Whispering to Anna one night as she leaves:

Do you want to start again, where we left off?

And Anna knows exactly what he means, she has been thinking the same thing – how else could she reply so quickly, so perfectly: Tuesday lunchtime.

And so it begins again.

Only this time, Sam finds he likes Anna. More than likes her, looks forward to seeing her.

One afternoon, sitting in the park with her on the walk back to the station and liking the way her hair shines in the light, feeling a tremor when he reaches out for her hand. Unexpected. Never expected to care.

Not sure when he first attaches the word love to the feeling that he has – but it is months before he tells her. A year maybe.

What is the point in her knowing? He has a family, so does she. And it works well as it is: one lunchtime a week.

Anna brings sandwiches with her (to save time). They do not always have a drink together afterwards. Sometimes

Sam has a meeting planned or an experiment. Anna never makes a fuss.

Loving Anna. Not with the fierce, biting, all-or-nothing love he feels for Pia. Not with the anxious, gnawing, silent love he feels for his son. No, this love is a light love.

Sam does not use the word. Because he doesn't have to.

I'd leave Steve for you – one day Anna tells him. If you asked me, if you wanted.

Rain. Loud rain, falling in lines in front of the window. A squirrel crouching on the bird table. Puddles changing as Marie looks as them. Imagining the drowning of ants, so many tiny things.

Sam does not come home and she does not miss him, but she misses someone. Something.

Crisp packets and biscuit wrappers, chocolate foil and banana skins. Television blaring, blaring and the woman inside the picture looks as if she is unhappy, but she does not know unhappy, not like Marie knows it.

A black bird in the tree, a crow, its head pivoting and still the rain falls and the grass is sodden. Yellow dandelion heads still standing but beginning to shake. The drooping roses, bedraggled as dresses soaked through. And the noise. Like the sky is speaking.

It's not right for her to be sitting alone like this night after night. Marie squeezes a handful of the pink flesh at the top of her thigh, watches it whiten and then pink again.

It's not that she wants Sam, but Anna does not know that and it is a – she likes the word, the scope, scale and sheer size of it, of what has been done to her, left alone here night after night – betrayal.

She has every right to scream.

Scream from the bottom of the stairs right up to the top.

The walls of the house shake, of that Pia is convinced, the cement between the bricks feeling crumbly, nervous. Each one of those bricks would run, she is certain, run if they could to get away.

Pia does not want to go down but each moment that she stays away she is making her mother more angry.

Calling: coming Mummy

Although her bladder burns and she has to squeeze her legs tight together, swinging her legs from the bed to the floor, feeling the cold linoleum under every step.

Calling out: coming Mummy, I am coming.

Starting to run now that she is closer, so she won't be punished for being too slow.

Marie is standing at the bottom of the stairs in a blue dressing gown and her hair is billowing out from the sides of her head like yellow fire. The air around her is shaking.

You didn't come quickly enough.

Smacking Pia once, hard, around the ear and the side of her face.

Pia feels her cheek burning and a film of tears across her eyes.

Did you hear me calling you?

Saying: yes Mummy.

And did you come immediately?

I tried to.

But?

But – I was asleep.

And now Marie is screaming at the grey-faced child. Hitting at the grey stick of her arm, the unmoving grey sticks of her ankles and legs.

You make me so angry. All your fault. All of it.

When Pia tries to run away, it makes Marie more angry. Slamming Pia's bedroom door before she has a chance to run inside of it.

Pia curls in on herself while the hands rain down.

pairing

Thirteen years later:

Marie is hitting. Hitting and hitting and Pia is calling for Sam.

Sam.

He is standing in the doorway now to Pia's bedroom.

Stop it Marie.

Pulling on her arm.

Stop it. Stop it now.

Pulling her off.

A cut by Pia's eyes, another on her lip; on her cheekbone a dark bruise forming.

Sitting on the edge of the bath with Sam. Sam dabbing at Pia's face with a ball of wet cotton wool.

It's not her fault. She can't help it. Marie is – Sam stops patting Pia's cheek and pulls back to look at her, searching for words – Marie is the most unhappy person, he says. Sometimes I think she is the most unhappy person in the world.

Marie is hitting. Hitting and hitting and Pia is calling for him:

Sam

And he is pulling Marie off Pia but angry now, he is angry.

Day after day. The pair of you. I can't concentrate with the two of you always quarrelling.

Eyes blazing at both of them.

I didn't do anything, Pia says quietly.

Always got an answer for everything, Marie says.

And Sam walks away.

He walks away.

The second time Sam walks away – walks out of the front door and into his car – it is easier. Closing the door behind him. Walking away.

Luke is around. Always. Afterwards. In Pia's bedroom. Or his. Not always touching her. Not always talking with Pia. But there. Always.

From the first moment, the first sighting of him, lying in Marie's arms. The softest thing Pia had ever seen and – reaching a finger out to touch his cheek – the warmest. Like his warmth travelled through his cheek and up into her finger, her wrist, her arm so that his heat was inside of her – even after she had left the room and was sitting in the corridor, swinging her legs backwards and forwards against the leg of the chair and hugging to herself the bright green water pistol Sam had bought for her on the way into the hospital because—

Today is a special day – he had told her, bringing his eyes

level with hers and she could see that he was feeling happy, that he wanted her to share it – you are going to meet your brother.

Brother.

He could not have known what she would feel when she sat out there in the corridor afterwards.

Bound to Luke. Though she never said a word to anyone. Not even to him.

And there was only him. After that. Always.

At first when Pia and Luke touched and it felt good, it was only that – good. A game between them in the field where the grass was long. There was nothing ugly in it, nothing painful. It just was what it was.

When Luke told a friend the things he did with his sister, he was eight years old. The friend wanted a go too, but Pia said no. Luke was glad she said no. Told his friend to find somebody else's sister

In the shed, in the fields, up against the wall. Before Pia wore a bra and then, after, sliding his hand up under the band to feel her. Makes him feel less edgy. The rest of the time there is the running. Feeling in a hundred pieces. And then Pia.

Always Pia.

Why do you want to spend so much time with your sister? the other boys ask him. And: why does she do boy things?

Because Pia hangs around with him in the playground and

she scores better goals than any of the others, knows all the right moves, her skinny legs and bony knees driving the ball home time after time.

Pia thinks: it is as if someone took a rope and bound us together – arms, ankles, thighs.

Made of the same stuff, thinks Pia, so there are no edges between us, no hard lines, no point at which you can say I end and he begins.

Luke says: it is too close, too much, we are inside each other's heads like a conversation. We are around each other's bodies like extra skin.

He cannot explain it to her.

She cannot understand.

The others mean nothing to him. Cissy girls with their magazines and whispers. Teases all of them. Stiff hair and melting arms. Wanting it like this, but not like that, going this far—

But – wriggling in his arms – no further.

Leaving lip-gloss on plastic cups. Leaning across pool tables, or sitting, crossing Immac-ed legs. They take it in turns to meet the boys out the back. A different one every week or so, going a little further every week or so.

Then speaking about it afterwards, in white-tiled toilets, spraying on perfume, oiling lips, wiping salivaed fingers under blue-smudged eyes. What they let him do, how it felt, what they did back.

Luke doesn't know why his friends bother. Though he does too, sometimes. Likes to smell their flower perfume, feel their plump flesh, whisper: HelenMichelleLouise. They all feel the same.

Pia steals. Sweets, pens, magazines. Lipsticks, mascaras, round plastic pots of pastes. She likes the feeling of picking something up, knowing it is not hers, deciding to have it and then taking it. Hiding it in her hand or her bag or her pocket, feeling it there, knowing it is not hers, walking towards the door and out into the street where there are people who do not know that when she takes it out of her pocket (handbag) it is not hers. But no one now is going to take it away.

Pia's drawers at home are crammed with things she does not use: bubble baths in plastic animal shapes (Pia likes the colours), furry toys (she likes the colours and the way they feel), packets of sweets and crisps and playing cards. Cigarette lighters, batteries and gardening tools. They spill on to the floor and are crammed under the bed.

With the girls, Pia either says nothing or she says too much and the silence afterwards is always uncomfortable. She wears clothes that make her invisible or else strange concoctions that make them want to stay away in case anyone thinks they are with her.

She is hard as nails, says Chloe. As stone. As a brick wall with another brick wall behind it. Yet you always sense she is about to cry and when she does she will cry for ever.

She writes long, complicated stories that the teachers pin in columns across the walls but when they try to talk to her she is monosyllabic at best, and very often silent. She shows them everything but keeps it all hidden away.

Luke is out in the car park under the lamps. Rolling skinny joints with one hand and writing words in the dust on cars with the other: prick, dope, cruise. He writes the words in fat thumb letters. On windscreens. On bonnets. On roofs. Pia is trailing round the car park behind him, not speaking much, just knocking against him, feeling close.

Like a boy, she is. Skinny and straight up and down like a board.

Stop following me around. Once he told her.

So she quit and he had to go looking for her.

Found her by the river. She wouldn't speak to him for an hour. *An hour.* But when she came round again, smiling up at him but also punching, lightly punching the base of his spine with her fist, he kissed her, to let her know he was sorry and she hung on to him like something drowning, just for a moment before pulling away.

Dirty dark green anorak. Why can't she wear something more appealing? Colour her face like the other girls. Sometimes just say: yes, I agree.

Chloe was after you tonight, Pia says.

I know.

What did you tell her?

To find someone else.

Why?

Pia is hanging back, shuffling, wanting to hear she's the only one, the best one, for ever.

Hearing nothing.

And then: not in the mood, he says.

Stopping now to face her, stroking her cheek, pulling her against him hard like a blanket in the night.

But it is like he is ashamed. Sometimes she thinks he is. Like she is dirty or bad. Like she has to be kept a secret. She knows why, of course. But that doesn't stop it hurting. Doesn't make the hole in her belly go away.

Marie grabs Pia in the hall and starts hitting her about the head and Pia pushes her just once, hard. Marie staggering back against the wall and stumbling on the stairs, missing a step or two backwards, falling away from Pia.

She could kill Marie. Sees herself doing it. Table lamp or Sam's paperweight. Dropping it on to her head. Or a pillow – Pia saw it in a film – a few kicks, arms thrashing, a muffled kind of scream – easy to drown. No one would know.

The other girls call Pia queer and ugly, running up behind her in the playground and pushing her.

Once, just once, they knock her to the ground. Fists raised in the centre of a group, all of them laughing. She scratches the face of the ringleader – Chloe – hair so white and straight and bright you might think she was an angel – if you were stupid, thinks Pia, really, really stupid.

Pia never thought Luke was stupid and yet there he is smiling up at Chloe while she twirls her hair through her fingers and bites on her lip. Small white teeth. No spots, no bruises. Surely he cannot be seeing just that – Pia standing a foot or so away kicking at the gravel with her plimsoll.

Luke is writing Chloe's telephone number on the back of his hand and Pia can hear him calling out to her—

I will ring you later.

Ring you later.

She cannot believe what she is hearing. Telling herself it is a mistake. For what reason would he want to telephone Chloe? What can she have to say that he could possibly want to hear?

Pia is standing with her back against a tree. The long grasses all around her are being flattened by the cool wind that sits inside her clothes like another layer of skin. Digging her nails into the bark of the tree and feeling a soft layer peeling away with her, rooting itself under her nails so that her fingers feel thick and fat at the ends. Pia imagines the tree under her nails rooting her legs into the earth.

She doesn't know how long she stays there. Watches the sky darken. Hears the quietening of birds and then the rustlings, the shifting leaves and grasses, the creaking of the trees.

Luke comes for her. Lights a cigarette for her in the darkness.

She walks back behind him, matching his fast steps, hearing their echo on the pavement.

Pia and Luke don't speak to each other for a week, living in the same house, using the same bathroom, walking the same routes.

Marie does not notice.

Sam, so often silent now behind his newspaper, is similarly unaware.

The invisible man – that's what Marie calls him, pulling his paper away from him and stamping it into the floor.

What about me?

You must ask that question fifty times a day, says Sam, or more. Adding: more – in a hundred silent ways.

He pays for new dresses, cinema outings, cigarettes and gin. Staring hard sometimes at the children he has been losing for years. Years since he held them in his arms and felt that they needed him, that he was important in their lives, the one they asked questions of.

Remembering: how far away is the moon? Is the earth made of fire? When I die will I be eaten by worms?

Sitting them on his lap, he told them stories in which all

the information was true so that they could learn about the world and not be afraid of it.

It happens like this ... and there would be a stream of words and he felt he was doing a mental jigsaw, putting all the pieces in the right places and then exhibiting for them a perfect pattern, an exact picture, an image they could recognise straight away.

Except they do not. Not any more.

Don't you see? he exclaims excitedly, it's only when the molecules collide in suspension and—

He can see by the looks on their faces, eyes glancing out of the window, fingers pulling together and apart, that all the words sound the same now and they don't care about their meaning.

Wanting to shake the pair of them.

Have you no idea of what is important?

Years now – he's sure – since Marie hit her, but Pia still walks round like a hunted animal, like any minute something might jump out at her, like she needs always to be on her guard.

Sam saying: I'm sorry.

Reaching out to touch her.

I didn't mean to frighten you.

Touching her arm but feeling there is no one in there and letting go of it instantly, not sure which of them feels the most afraid.

feeling like a stranger

Sam's father is dying.

His mother sends a note: your father says he will see you.

Sam imagines the old man dictating the words to her. Not: wants to see; or would like to see; but will – thinks Sam. He has not changed a bit.

I will not go, thinks Sam.

And for a moment he enjoys the illusion: being the one to finally shut the door.

Sam telephones his mother an hour after receiving the letter, says:

I can drive down tonight.

Yes, his mother says. I think he would like that.

And you?

Me? Why are you asking about me?

Because you matter.

Matter? his mother says. There is nothing the matter with me.

Travelling to his father's house in a swirling mist, Sam takes a wrong turn and ends up driving through a housing estate. A few people moving. Dark shapes in the shifting white.

He takes another wrong turn. And another.

Lost and all the roads look the same, sound the same: names of composers. Lost in Beethoven Mews, looking for Mozart Street.

Feeling suddenly that the car is too small. Much too small. Foot down hard on the accelerator, screeching, turning miserably. Round in noisy circles.

Suddenly seeing the main road again, Sam's heart leaping with relief.

And parking outside his father's house, he chastises himself for his panic. A few wrong turns, a bit of mist and feeling like a stranger. What had there been to feel frightened about?

Knocking firmly, loudly on the door. Hearing his mother's footsteps in the hall.

Don't make him excited, she says.

Don't worry.

He is very ill.

I know.

Halfway up the stairs, Sam's mother starts shaking. Noiselessly. Head slumping on to her chest. Whole body shaking.

Sam is standing two steps below her on the stairs.

Are you all right?

(Unable to touch her.)

Then a sound escapes from his mother. And another. And another. She is screaming.

He can't die. I won't let him. What will I do without him?

Nothing could have prepared Sam. No verbal description—

So ill, his mother said, so weak.

Nothing could have prepared him for this sack of cloth and bones. His father collapsing in on himself like a tent without a guy rope. And the hacking. The wheezing sound of his breath.

Sam is here to see you.

Lizard eyes. His father has the skin of a reptile. Shiny at the wrists where his night shirt ends. Propped up on pillows. Head dropping over to one side.

Hello, Sam says.

And for a moment the commotion stops as his father looks at him, then it begins again. A rattle and gurgle deep in his chest.

He can't speak, says Sam's mother.

How long?

Long?

How long has he been like this?

Three years, she says. Every time I suggested we tell you he said no. No, she says. Even after he could say it with words, saying it with his eyes – I can still read his eyes. And then yesterday, suddenly, he told me to tell you to come.

And now? What is he saying now?

Sam's mother bends down and looks closely at her husband's eyes.

He wants you to leave, she says.

His final joke, thinks Sam, his final humiliation. One final rejection so the old man can go out in style.

I wanted to be close to him, thinks Sam, just for a moment.

Idiot – inside his head he hears his father's voice.

———————————

Standing in the graveyard, watching men shovel earth on top of the old man's head.

Back at the house, Sam's mother is tiny. Crouching over her handbag, accepting cake from a neighbour but leaving it unnoticed on her plate.

Sunlight bounces off the window in the roof of the shed and into the lounge. Figures hunched over tea plates. Quiet clatter of cup against saucer and knife against plate.

You could hear a crumb fall – Sam wants to laugh. To run to the top of the hall steps and laugh.

Gone. The old man is gone. Like a tree in a garden covering a patch of grass with shade. When you cut the tree down, the grass sees sunlight.

Seeing sunlight. Bouncing off the roof of the shed and dazzling in his eyes.

Marie picks up the television guide. Sees Selina's pencil circles round programmes she would like to see: golfing highlights, wildlife documentaries and afternoon quiz shows.

He liked to watch them, Selina says. Even at the end.

No tears now, Selina thinks, just a dryness like a desert. An aching desert.

The chair where he used to sit and his cup and his glasses – and his spare teeth in the cabinet next to the extra bar of soap. What is she to do with it all?

Drawers and cupboards, a shed and a garage full of it. No use for any of it any more. And no use for her.

What am I supposed to do now? Nothing feels real. Too enormous. The thought that he is gone.

And clothes to be worn, nights to be slept through, food to be eaten.

And no desire now to do any of it. What purpose in plumping up the pillows and making the bed? Or buying a fresh piece of fish or a bag of currant buns? What point in taking another breath?

Doing it automatically – the way she will learn to do all those other things – the cooking, cleaning, tidying, walking that tell other people she is alive.

You could take a holiday, Sam says. In a month or so, when this is all over.

He might as well be speaking a foreign language – holiday, month, over – what does any of it mean? As if this will ever be over? As if there will every be anything else?

No book, no film, no place, no person, no taste, no smell to please her.

Sam takes his mother fresh cream cakes and sandwiches crammed with ham and cheese. Long boxes of chocolates and fresh fruits in paper bags. He finds them melted and rotten a week later exactly where he left them in the hall.

She is disappearing. A little less of her each time he visits. Clothes a little baggier, gathering in folds round her arms.

Is there anything you want?

Always the same question, always the same answer.

No nothing – or perhaps—

Sam hovers at the door.

No, nothing, she says.

Instead of life, Sam's mother has this: a room with a television and a gas fire and a clock.

She likes to look at photographs of her husband. As he used to be. She likes to remember.

He was a good man, she says. One of the few good men. I was lucky to have him. You were lucky to have him.

And Sam listens though his insides jump. You should not be allowed to tell such lies about the dead – Sam thinks – when the dead are no longer here to prove otherwise.

Sam never expected to miss the old man. But he wakes in the middle of the night because he hears him speaking. Jolting him out of his sleep. Suddenly smelling the soap on his razor, the smell of him straight out of the shower. After all these years.

tracing
a tree

Chloe says: Pia could be pretty if she did something with her hair.

So Pia lets Chloe colour her face and put dye on her hair. Sitting in Chloe's bedroom that is pink and white lace and, for a moment, Pia craves it – all this confectionery – and the feelings that go with it.

There are rows of boots and shoes standing next to each other in Chloe's wardrobe, scarves and belts on hangers, rows of blouses and dresses ranged according to colour so that they run a rainbow spectrum – splash of yellow, then pink, then green.

How do you decide what to wear?

It depends on my mood, says Chloe, and how I want to feel.

Choosing how you want to feel – Pia is impressed with the possibility – and by the idea: wearing a red jumper (happy colour) or a blue dress (for more sombre moods).

Pia tries it for a while.

Luke still speaks to Chloe on the telephone using a voice Pia does not know; he still tells Chloe stories on street corners, still takes her to the cinema, passes toffees and boiled sweets from his mouth to hers.

Waiting for Luke to come home. Car headlamps lighting up the curtains, the bed, the ashtray spewing butts.

The creaking of the floorboards in the hall by the bathroom, the whisper-sound of Luke peeing, shuffling, creeping into his bedroom. And lying there, alone in the darkness, but seeing every move and gesture that he makes.

Sometimes he comes to get Pia, staggering across the hall and collapsing on to her bed.

The room is swimming.

Giggling.

Swim with me.

Touching her.

Who else have you been touching? (Trying not to say it.)

Sometimes she stays in her bedroom, mind stretched tight like the skin of a drum and limbs clenching. *I will not go in there, will not show I care.* More often, after counting to a hundred perhaps or fifty or ten, she pads across the hall towards him, slips into the bed beside him, breathes in his alcohol haze.

So many times they nearly do but Pia says no – at the last minute. So many times.

It does not feel right.

Feeling him hunching away from her.

I want the first time to be special.

Setting a date for it – Pia's birthday. Four months away.

After Chloe there is Juliette. Then Bea, then Lindsey.

And in between and during there is Pia.

It is not that she forgives him.

It is not that she forgets them – faces like a gallery of horrors in her head, each slightly more deadly than the one before.

It is just that when she is with him, she no longer feels alone.

It is an afternoon in winter. Pia and Luke have just got home from school. Pia is at the kitchen table spreading toast with sandwich spread and peanut butter, while Luke sits on the sideboard, swinging his legs backwards and forwards, smoking a cigarette. She makes a cup of tea and he watches her as she moves around the kitchen.

When is Marie due back?

Not until after seven.

And Sam?

An hour after that.

Luke smiles at Pia and she feels her colour rising. Sometimes he feels like a stranger to her. Though she knows him and the thoughts he is thinking. Sometimes it feels as if the space between them is the size of an ice rink, other times there is no space at all.

In his room, they turn on the radio. Listen to a woman

announcing there will be rain and almost instantly they hear it, bouncing off the roof and the windows, hissing through the trees.

A storm.

A low dark grumble.

Watching the sky crack apart.

It's God, he says, with a bellyache.

They stand at the window. Watching the garden shake and split.

It is Pia's idea to go out into the garden. Taking Luke by the hand and pulling him down the stairs.

Coats, he says.

No.

Yes – grabbing his jacket off the back of the chair. I'm not sure I want to do this.

He stands on the back step, hand out into the downpour.

No, he says.

But she pulls him quickly outside. Standing under the water, arms outstretched.

You can feel the earth tremble, she says.

We could be standing at the end of the world.

Back inside, stripping off sodden clothes. Puddles from the back door through the kitchen and up the stairs. Clusters of socks, trousers and a skirt, a shirt with the tie still wound round.

Luke says: the last one into the room and naked takes a dare.

Tumbling, pushing. Wet hair on cold skin. The rasp of carpet underfoot.

Luke grabs Pia by the ankles and pulls her backwards. She wriggles out of his hands, into his room and slams the door.

I won.

You've still got your necklace on.

So?

He is standing in the doorway looking at her. She is cross-legged on his bed, hair dripping on to the bedspread.

I win.

No you don't.

Yes I do.

Parading in the doorway. His white skin, dark hair, the curves and lines of his back.

So you get a forfeit, he says.

All right, what is it?

He springs across the room, lands on the bed beside her.

I'll keep it in my bank, he says. One more thing you have to do for me.

His bank. The one in his head. Profit and loss. A list of trade-offs and bets. Who owes him what and why. Because one day Luke wants to be rich. Very rich. To have everything I want, he says. To feel completely and utterly satisfied.

How overdrawn am I today?

Seventy-two.

Seventy-two?

You owe me seventy-two favours.

How will I pay them all?

You have your whole life, he says.

Pia gets a towel from the bathroom to dry her hair. Luke wants to draw a picture on Pia's body so she lies face down on the bed, head twisting round as the biro nib tickles across her back.

What are you drawing?

You.

Me?

And me, in the rain. See, here is a tree.

He starts tracing his pen lines with his finger.

And this is you.

His hand moves in a swirl and this, moving lower, this is me.

Turning round and arching up towards him, the cold dampness of his belly, rainwater still on his neck. His fingers moving and hers, hers up and down his back, his arms, his chest.

Does it feel like this with the others?

You know, Luke says the words into her hair. You know that it does not.

At first, they do not see her. The woman standing in the doorway still in her coat and scarf. She has dropped her bag of shopping and her black leather handbag and she is standing there holding Pia's school tights and one of Luke's wet socks. She does not speak. There are no words. Just the vision of her son's back and bottom and her daughter's arms and legs. Like they are all in the wrong order, her arms in his shoulders, his legs on her hips. But it is not the order that is wrong, they are all in the wrong place.

Wrong, wrong, wrong.

Oh my God.

Marie biting on her glove and the damp wool tastes of metal.

Pia, she shouts. Luke.

And even then it takes a moment for them to turn round.

Pia covers herself with the duvet, pulling it up towards her neck.

This cannot be happening.

Cannot.

Wanting to bang their wicked heads against the walls, wanting to run out on to the street and pretend she has seen nothing. Wanting to keep walking down that street, and walking, away from everything.

family

Marie is crying in the lounge.

What's the matter?

Sam walks in to the house to find her there.

Are you all right Marie?

She is not able to talk. Bursting into fresh sobs each time she looks at him or opens her mouth.

Eventually he asks: is it the children?

Yes – she screams the word at him. Yes, it's the children. If you could have seen them. If you could only have seen—

Seen what?

Sam is running his hand through his hair, coming to sit on the other armchair.

You're away so much and you leave it all to me. I can't watch them twenty-four hours a day.

No one expects you to.

Twisted devils.

You are not making sense.

Sex. Marie spits the word out.

Have you caught one of them—?

Both.

What has happened? Marie tell me.

Pia and Luke.

Yes?

Luke and Pia.

Yes.

Don't you get it?

No, says Sam, exasperated. I don't get it.

Having sex.

The words tumble out now like a dam has suddenly given way.

In Luke's bedroom. I saw them. I saw them having sex.

Sam cannot believe it. Will not believe it. He looks at the lampshades and curtains – the colours and patterns that they chose, the three-seater settee and matching armchair, the low table for coffee, the coasters for hot cups. It all looks the way it does in other houses and yet—

Sam says: you are lying.

Why would I lie? Ask them, she says, if you don't believe me.

Marie's face is puffed and streaked with tears.

Ask them what they get up to when we are out of the house.

Sam sweeps his arm across a shelf decorated with Marie's trinkets, sending pots and china animals crashing, landing in a broken fountain at his feet. He is grateful for the sound. The crashing. It is as if the world is standing still for a moment – no going back in time, but no moving forward either – in that shiver splinter of sound.

What are we to do? What are we to do?

Over and over, Marie's words bang against Sam's head likes a child's ball against a wall.

Finally yelling at her. I don't know, for God's sake. How am I supposed to know what to do? You started all of this.

All of what?

All the twisting, Sam shouts. You and your lies and your inability to love. I blame you.

After all these years, finally saying it.

Me?

Yes.

And it is as if a new Sam steps out of the old one and stands there in front of her.

I blame you, he says. I should have known, he says, should have expected. How could anything that came out of you be straight?

Straight?

Straight, he says, straight, not bent, not crooked. Everything about you – so close to her now his breath is hot in her face. From the night I first met you, he says, you lied to me. And I fell for you because you were easy.

Easy?

Easy and cheap.

Sam says: if the children are twisted it is because they have a mother who does not love them.

And a father – shrieks Marie – who is never at home.

What is there to be at home for? Sam sneers. And what about it makes it homely?

We're a *family*, Marie says.

She manages to make the word sound like barbed wire. And it sits there between them, two syllables with *ill* inside.

Sam vomits in the toilet bowl. One hand to his head, the other pressed against the cold tile wall.

Sam blames Marie. Blames her so utterly it is as if the whole thing is happening to someone else. Not him.

The numbness lasts for two days. Enabling Sam to talk civilly to Pia and Luke as he passes them on the stairs.

On the third day Sam cracks. Shudders of rage coursing up and down his body, sending him running into Luke's bedroom where the boy is sitting, pulling him up by the collar of his T-shirt and twisting his arm up behind his back.

You little bastard.

Luke twists in his father's grasp, but his father holds on.

You dirty, scheming little—

Luke's eyes when Sam catches sight of them are expressionless and flat.

You don't care about anyone but yourself. Your needs, hisses Sam. Your wants. Selfish, self-centred little—

And who do you think I learned it from?

Luke's voice, when he speaks, is as expressionless as his eyes.

What sort of a father do you think you've been? Someone to look up to on the rare occasions you've been here? Luke sucks in his breath. I don't think so.

Sam remembers the first time he picked Luke up, held him close. Their son, his son, his. Hello little boy, he said. But he could have been holding a bag of oranges or a pillow or a small dog for all the emotion he felt for the bundle in his arms.

Sam thought it would get better, as the boy got older, learned to walk and talk a bit, became a little man. But Luke was always a little stranger. Running between his legs and tugging on his arm.

And the ship mobile in his drawer. Still in his drawer. As if, some day—

Sam feels his shell cracking like an edge of fired clay.

Wanting to say: Luke I tried.

Sam feels his father's head sitting on his shoulders, his father's punching hands.

How many times did the old man tell Sam – you're useless, what are you?

Useless, Sam would say, I'm useless.

And you owe me everything you've got. What do you owe me?

I owe you everything.

Don't you forget it.

And all the time hating him.

Feeling Luke's hatred now. One hand hooked still into his T-shirt, his son dangling off it like a bedraggled piece of cloth.

Letting go of him, surprised the boneless boy does not collapse into a heap on the floor, but stays standing there instead, almost on top of Sam's toes, swaying there in front of him.

Pia says: we can't help it.

And she says: you don't understand, what we feel, how strong it is.

Luke stands in the doorway, not speaking, not leaving, but disappearing inside.

Pia cannot turn to Luke and say: tell them. She can only look at the side of his head and his body and think: get me out of here, take me away.

Marie wakes in the middle of the night to see her children's faces blurring and reshaping in front of her. Pia with Luke's nose. Luke with Pia's mouth. One set of arms between them. Fish tails for legs.

In her dreams they say: it is because of you Marie. That's why your children have turned in on themselves. It is because of the lies you told.

Marie wants Pia and Luke to turn their feelings off like a tap.

All it takes is willpower, she says, and the realisation that your feelings are wrong.

Luke, she says. Pia. You must stop.

Trying to stop.

It is not willpower that it takes. Not stamina, not resolve. Stopping loving Luke requires a switching off of the senses, a short, sharp deadening of the perceptions so that everything is muted and nothing is clear. Pia learns to unfocus her eyes, to switch her view from looking at to looking through. And her body, she can turn it into blancmange, wobbly and pink and shapeless, as she passes him on the stairs or in the kitchen.

Smelling apples, wood, the smoke-scent of his hair.

Then bumping into him in the garden. It is three o'clock in the morning, both of them needing the sharp, black air, and it is the suddenness of the contact, the warm sudden feel of him, there is no decision to move or not move, just the feel of him again, the feeling she has always known.

He is with her then. With her against Marie. She wants to climb inside his pocket, wants it to be a house they can both live inside.

pictures

Marie sends Pia away. Away from Luke. To stay with her sister who lives by the sea.

Aunt Sylvie – who knows all the facts because she is their mother's sister – and Sylvie's son Gerard, who does not.

Because the less people who know, the better, says Marie. Thinking: better it had never happened at all. Craving only a kind of normality. Knowing now there are shades even of that.

Sam goes to see Pia the night before she is leaving. Sits on her bed and watches as she bundles her belongings into bulging bags.

Won't be for long, he says. And then you can come back. There are plenty of boys out there Pia – wanting to reach out to her. A whole world of boys and opportunities.

Thinking about his opportunities, the ones he watched disappear. Wanting that world of opportunities for her, saying:

Don't throw it all away.

I'm not, says Pia. I'm not throwing anything away. It's you – you and Marie – throwing me away.

Being thrown away, Sam says, is that what it feels like?

He stands up but sits down again immediately. Grateful for the solid feel of the bed beneath his legs.

I don't know what else to do, he says.

Luke stays out the night before Pia leaves.

She looks all over for him in the morning, doesn't want to leave without saying goodbye.

But – loading her bags into the car – grateful not to see his eyes.

Luke bangs around the house without Pia in it. So much empty space. Curling into a ball on his bed. Barricading the door with his chest of drawers. The stairs seem wide, the lounge long, the kitchen gaping.

When is she coming back?

It's only been a week, says Marie. She won't be back for a long time.

Luke and Melanie, Sally, Yvonne, Patricia. Two one night and three the next – then meeting Vanessa in the alley between his house and hers.

And, just for a moment, to get lost inside of someone else.

How to keep away from Pia for a lifetime? How to manage one more day?

Marie sees herself as a wall with arms. She is a wall between her children and her arms are pushing and pushing them apart. At night they jump over and run amok around her, when her arms feel weak and she begins to sag.

Must remain vigilant. She reminds herself on waking. Checking the post. Always being the first to the telephone.

The two halves of her life are clashing, banging and crashing into each other. She must keep them apart.

Sam is Marie's ally. Pulled together with a common aim, a shared belief.

One night she roasts a chicken for him, finds herself opening a bottle of wine.

I might lose weight, she says, standing up to clear the plates from the table. I'm thinking about it, she says.

Then: would you like that?

What?

Would you like it if I was slim again?

Marie, Sam says very slowly, we've gone too far for that.

He is standing up, walking towards the door, saying: too far, too long. It could never work.

You don't know. How can you be sure?

Sam says: because I never loved you.

There are levels, Marie thinks, to which a person should never sink.

Not for one moment? – she has to ask him.

No, Sam says, not for one.

Pia writes Luke a letter, sends it care of his friend Midge.

Luke sends Pia a cigarette card, a hello scribble on a scrap of paper, a set of wooden dice and three-quarters of a chocolate bar.

One night, when Sam telephones Pia, Luke is passing in the hall, on his way out, so Sam hands him the receiver – although it is against Marie's dictates.

Doing all right?

Pia breathes the words into the mouthpiece.

Doing fine – she sounds as if she is floating. Wishing you were here.

The rest of the time, there is cousin Gerard. Never far away.

I know what you're here for.

What?

You love your brother.

What?

I heard our mothers talking – coming too close – I know what you do.

And knowing what she did makes Gerard tingle. Like a tiny fuse has been lit at the base of his spine and is fizzing slowly all the way to his head where there are pictures: Pia and Luke, Pia and him.

Gerard watches Pia climbing across the rocks and down to the sea, her legs skimming the stones, fingers holding on and moving.

He imagines it all again in his head at night, lying on his back on his bed, listening to the noise of the trees: sea, Pia's legs, stones, Pia's fingers.

And again the next day

And the next night.

Seen so many times – the freckles on her arm, the white line of down on her neck, the red and shiny insect bite by the side of her elbow. Some days it seems there is no distinction between looking at her and touching her. Who could say, when he reaches out his fingers and feels her there in front of him, whether it is part of his dream or as solid as the stones.

But she will not let him touch her and that makes him angry.

Slag, he calls. Slut.

Puffing and panting as he climbs the stones behind her, red in the face, sweating too.

Pia is laughing at him, running into the wind, her anorak puffing out behind her like an inflatable wing. He wants to punch her. For laughing. For being faster. For having something that he wants.

Bitch – even though she is far away now and can't possibly hear him – whorecowbitch.

Scrambling up the rocks, feeling wide as a mountain, chest choking.

Whorecowbitch.

Palms grazed and stinging with the salt. She makes him feel ugly.

Running to catch up, blown about by the wind, ragged as the tops of trees.

Wait.

Seeing her running, the black flashes of her legs, hair catching the light.

He wants to show her. *Show her.* Writing him off every time she looks at him. Bitch.

Pia is sitting on the rocks, back pressed against the remains of an old tower. Wet red bricks, old newspapers and fag ends inside. She is looking out at the sea, grey churning waves, white tipped, and the birds swooping and soaring.

Staring out at the sea, how still she looks, wind whipping up the sand on the rocks around her and her hair flying loose from its band. Not moving. The rough red of her hands, heart-shaped mole on her cheek.

Gerard is sitting beside her quietly. Wanting only that. But she is getting up to go, now that he is here and he is saying:

Wait.

Why?

I want to talk to you.

What about?

About the rocks, he says. I know where fossils are.

So?

Millions of years old.

So?

I can take you to them.

No thanks.

And she is doing it again, dismissing him, like he is nothing.

Grabbing hold of her wrist, liking the feeling, the way it slips and twists inside his fingers like a fish.

Let me go.

Holding on tighter, grabbing her other hand as it smacks against him. Both her wrists now inside of one hand and she is bucking, kicking.

Let go of me.

She is breathless.

Let go.

Then her eyes, suddenly, so close to his eyes. Not clawing at him now, not struggling but with a meanness.

What are you holding on to me for? Teasing. What are you going to do?

Tell me what you do.

Who?

You and your brother.

She twists inside his grasp and she could be dancing. His hands could be a rope. She smells of perfume oil and dirty hair.

Tell me.

No.

Like Luke has something special. Like Gerard has nothing, is nothing. No one has the right to make him feel like that.

Grabbing at the zip of her anorak, her sweatshirt, up and under all those layers and she feels different from the way he had imagined, less soft, less smooth, but warmer. Fumbling with the zip of her jeans, doing it all so quickly and all he is really thinking about is holding down her elbows, knees hard against her knees, pinning her there, jabbing it in now, in, because it is hard and she is there and coming like his whole body is an explosion, exploding inside of her.

Afterwards, he wants to lie there with her on the rocks by the old tower, touch her more gently, now that she is stiller, stroke her hair perhaps, her arms, her cheek. But she is wriggling away from him. Her anorak is making a scratchy sound on the stones. He thinks he can hear her crying.

Are you all right?

Beginning to feel he might have done—

I'm sorry—

Something awful.

Sitting up now, looking at her.

Pia, he says, I'm sorry.

Salt wind in her face. Running. Salt water running from her eyes and into her mouth and collecting in the coat-folds underneath her chin.

Running. Rocks shifting and changing under her feet.

Gerard is still attached to her. He is still inside of her.

Over the grey rocks and down to the sea, watching it heaving.

She didn't stop it, couldn't stop it.

Sea splashing, crashing.

Walking along the sand, picking up ring-pulls and shards of coloured glass, filling her hands and squeezing, seeing blood, spotting a trail. Knowing that should be hurting. But what does hurt feel like?

Walking out into the sea, knowing the water is climbing up her jeans, into her pockets, creeping up to her waist, her breasts, her neck. But what does wet feel like?

Moving one foot up forward down, other foot up forward down and not stumbling, but gliding, through the cold air. A connection, somewhere, between head and foot but she has not put it there, could not have put it there, because she is a hundred miles away.

bad-hearted trouble

The police find Pia the next morning.

We followed spots of blood, one policeman tells the local newspaper. Asleep on the rocks, he says, whiskey bottle and cigarettes by her side.

A runaway.

Pia's aunt is buttering bread in the kitchen—

After all I have tried to do for you—

thin yellow creaming the floury white loaf.

Marie is right—

Tearing a hole in one of the slices of bread and seeing the wooden board through it like a stain—

Nothing but trouble.

Banging the knife on the table.

Bad-hearted trouble.

And – thinking of Pia's effect on Gerard – the loping, pining way he has been.

Sending her back to her parents.

She is too much to handle—

Handing her over.

And Gerard is different, says Aunt Sylvie. Since Pia arrived.

Pia holds on to Luke when she sees him. Holds on even though Sam and Marie are watching and their aunt and her son. Holds on to him in the hope he will feel solid.

Feeling the scratchy wool of his jumper, just for a moment, bringing back to life three fingers, a cheek and part of her lips, resting there against him. She can feel him.

Feel him as he pulls away from her.

Not now.

He says the words into her hair, so quiet no one else could have heard him. Running his finger along her arm.

We have time, he says.

Smiling.

She can feel him. She can feel.

Marie locks Pia in her bedroom.

What else, she says, am I to do? Wherever you go, she says, trouble, she says. And she is squeezing Pia's arm so tightly that Pia can see the imprint of her fingers.

Don't you think we've all – and Marie's breath is in Pia's face when she says *all* – wanted to run away? Don't you think I've wanted to walk out on you, you and your brother and the invisible man? Where do you think my good times come from? What makes you think my life's so great?

Pia says: I don't.

Skivvying around the three of you, stuck here and being – Marie slumps on to the bed, pulling at the flesh beneath her arms – and being so fat that even the invisible man finds someone else to give the dry pellets of his love. Do you know what that's like?

No, says Pia.

You think you're so great, says Marie. Think that your youth and your slim body will pave a bright future. Well let me tell you—

Standing in the doorway now, key in her hand—

There is no great future for you.

Late sun in the trees. Sam unlocks Pia's bedroom door and goes in there to see her.

Welcome back, he says. I've missed you.

Pia does not say anything.

You're only locked up, he says, until you and Luke can control it.

It – it has become the word they can all use and understand without causing a commotion.

It, Pia says.

Yes, Sam says, it.

Pia looks – the word that comes in to Sam's mind is – straggly. Sitting at her chair by the window, snags in her jumper, tangles in her hair.

Sam moves closer to Pia, reaches out his hand to stroke her but she is backing away from him and into the wall.

Don't touch me, she says.

Recoiling, seeing in her eyes a new expression, knowing

instantly that something is wrong but – hand still hovering in the air around her—

What is it?

Pia shrugs her shoulders.

Is something wrong? Are you all right?

Pia still does not answer.

We didn't throw you away, Sam says.

Pia sits on her bed and stares out of the window, out at the tops of trees where a tatty black bird is twitching.

The light fades.

When a stone hits her window, she shudders. Then there is another stone and another.

Opening the window and peering outside into the darkness. She can see Luke standing at the base of the tree. He shines his torch up at her. She sees the red stripes of his shirt, glint of gold in his ear and, for a moment, his eyes.

Pia finds her torch, jacket, shoes. Cigarettes and gum in her pocket. Runs her fingers through her hair.

Climbing out of the window, over the ledge and down the drainpipe. Slowly, carefully.

Feeling his hands around her waist, reaching up for her, pulling her down on to him. They collapse in a heap.

The feel of his fingers, hair, nose. The warm hard lines of his body. The way they fit together with hers.

Did you miss me?

Some of the time.

And the rest of the time?

I missed you, he says, isn't that enough? Pia was sent away and now she has been sent back.

I feel, she says, like a parcel with the wrong address. Or a letter to someone who has gone missing.

She wants to tell him about Gerard but they have so little time together and it feels so good just lying in the grass with him looking up at the stars.

She wants to tell him about the hole that is getting bigger, but although the sentences chase each other around her head, the words don't explain what happened and what happened doesn't explain the way she feels.

Bits of me are disappearing, she tells Luke, because she wants him to know something.

There is time, she thinks, to tell him. I will tell him in time.

But there is something about not speaking.

It has been a week, seven days and nights, one hundred and sixty-eight hours since Gerard became a part of her skin and the not-telling has become familiar. Like her favourite mauve jumper – the unchanging colour of it gives comfort.

Nobody knows what happened a week ago on the rocks. Except Gerard. And he isn't telling. What difference would it make if someone else knew? Telling can't take it away.

Yet when she is with Luke, sometimes, his skin next to her skin, she wonders if he feels it: that someone else is there.

And sometimes when she is with him, the words sit inside her mouth like splinters of glass. And she wants him to know, with every fibre of her being she wants him to know, but she doesn't want to speak.

Gerard comes at night. When everyone else is asleep. And he does it again. Again and again. He is two hundred miles away but he does it again. Inside Pia's bedroom, in between her sheets.

She wakes screaming. Kicking off bedclothes and running into walls.

Sometimes Luke wakes and whispers to her through the locked door.

What's going on?

Nothing.

What are you afraid of?

Daring to say it: Gerard.

Gerard? Luke starts to laugh. You cannot be serious. How can that lardy-boy scare you?

Pia thinks: there is a shame that comes with silence. The creeping feeling that, in not-telling (and not-telling and not-telling) you are telling a lie. Each time you say: nothing is wrong, or: I'm fine, or: I don't know what's the matter with me, you are lying.

The lies build like bricks. One day they are a huge, great wall.

There are days when she forgets.

There are days when she can think of nothing else.

There is a week in which Aunt Sylvie sends Marie a letter saying:

I think Gerard has got a girlfriend. He has started playing music in his bedroom. I found a poem in his diary, the beginnings of a letter by his bed.

There is a night when Luke says: two weeks to your birthday, two weeks to go. Because he still thinks there will be a first time for them both, together, and Pia starts crying, crying and crying.

Luke does not understand, feels shut out and then angry. Shouting at her, shouting:

If something is the matter with you then tell me. How can I help if you won't tell me what's wrong?

But mostly there is a numbness, a sense that everything is floating and is very far away.

a hundred
monkeys

Sam's mother does not kill herself with a knife. She does not use pills or a rope or a revolver. She does not put her head in the oven, under water, or by the exhaust from her dead husband's car. Sam's mother kills herself with lack of desire.

She slips from life to death without any visible sign. Sitting in the hospital with her, it takes Sam an hour, perhaps more, to notice that she is not moving – or rather the sheet across her chest is not moving. Another ten minutes to decide to call her softly:

mother.

Propped up on pillows, so he can see the whole of her face. Eyes closed. Her white skin creased in folds. Such tiny ears.

Walking over to the bed and – slowly – laying his hand upon her arm and feeling her cold there. Unnaturally cold.

Collapsing then into the chair beside her – how long since he has been this close to her? His mother slipping away from him minute by minute.

His mother, gone now, no more chances – and he never knew she had such tiny ears.

Luke wants to be inside Pia. It is the day they have agreed upon: twelfth of April, Pia's birthday.

Pia climbs out of her bedroom window and down the drainpipe. Meets Luke in the shed. He has brought a bottle of cider and a spliff, chocolate cake and digestive biscuits. Daylight is fading.

Come on, says Luke. Don't you want to do it?

Yes, says Pia. Yes.

They are lying on the floor of the shed, skeins of cobwebs and dust clinging to their jeans.

He stands up, unbuttoning his jeans, kicking off his shoes.

Come on.

Reaching out his hand to her, wanting to pull her to her feet.

What's the matter?

Nothing.

Doesn't look like nothing – half in, half out of his jeans, pouting, head on one side.

She is lying there as if her body is wood or stone. Just lying there looking up at him.

But he is pulling on her hand until she is standing, unzipping her jacket, lifting her sweatshirt up and over her arms. Bare arms and legs. The damp wood smell of his chest.

It is Luke beside her so why does it feel like Gerard?

Rain rattles on the roof. Sounds like a hundred monkeys.

Pushing him away, squeezing her eyes shut, squeezing her whole body into a knot like a fist.

Pia? – gently—

It is Luke's voice. It is Luke. Taking Gerard's place.

Knowing it is Luke.

Pia pulls him towards her, liking it now, the feeling of Luke slipping into her skin, seeping into her.

Luke's body is her own and her own is a part of his, reaching through the gaps between because there is no difference, no his no hers, no yours no mine.

Pia opens her eyes and sees Luke, the cobwebbed shed, his pale white skin and wonders why he is looking at her, frowning. She feels her face with the back of her hand, knowing then that it is wet and she is crying. Hearing the sobs now, surprised that they are coming out of her.

Did I hurt you?

No.

Then what is the matter?

And now is the time – if she can only find the words – Gerard sitting here with them in the shed, because he never goes away, never far away – opening her mouth to speak his name—

Suddenly Luke says: is it Gerard?

Looking so hard at her face, banging his hand against his head – how could I have been so stupid? How could I not have known? And: Pia I am sorry.

Sorry?

Luke says: the way you looked each time you spoke about him. The way you were, he says, you are, from the moment you got back.

And telling him.

Finally.

Finally.

And watching him shrink, like Gerard is doing it to him and it is hurting. Curling in on himself, knees up, head down.

Saying only: Pia, Pia. Over and over like a mantra.

Later he is angry. Pacing around the shed, bare feet on wood shavings and cigarette butts.

Luke is kicking a box to pieces, wanting to hurt Gerard or Sam or Marie – wanting to hurt himself most of all.

I'm going to find him.

Looking at Pia still crumpled there on the floor.

I've told you now, she says. It will be better.

And what if it's not? What about the nightmares?

They're not so bad.

What's the matter with you? Don't you want him to suffer?

I just want to stop thinking about it.

The idea comes to Luke slowly. Forms at the outer edges of his consciousness and creeps nearer and nearer—

run away—

what is there to stay for, what is stopping them?—
run away—
where to, what for, how will they live, eat, sleep?
What do you think?
What?
About it?
He had been imagining having the conversation with Pia in his head and all the time she was staring out the window, had not heard one word he had said.
Running away.
Where would we go?
Somewhere. Anywhere different.

It is a way out.
And it is a way to be together.

Pia says: I'm not sure, but all the time she is thinking yes.
She asks questions about money and transport, about the police and school and money again. But all the time she is not listening to his answers.
We'll manage, we'll be fine, steal a car, eat at service stations—
Pia is thinking about Gerard and the way she feels when she is with Luke. Pia is thinking of the lock on her door, and the thin line of Marie's mouth. Pia is thinking: get me out of here, take me away.

breastbone

Two rucksacks and three carrier bags: clothes and tapes and magazines.

Walking down the darkened street.

A street away, a car with the passenger door unlocked. Luke puts his bags inside, reaches under the dashboard for the ignition switch, hot-wires the engine.

Luke stands there. Rainwater like marbles on his leather jacket.

Shrugging. Standing there and shrugging.

Coming?

Pia is holding on to his jacket, half running behind him and into the car. Swinging her legs in and the cough of the heater, too hot then too cold.

Luke leans over to put a cassette in the recorder, handing Pia a cigarette he has lit.

Everything is black: the houses, the trees, the gardens. Speeding into the darkness. Loud purring engine. The dashboard casts green shadows and Pia doesn't care how far they go or for how long. There is nothing she needs that is outside of the car.

Black coffee in polystyrene cups. Sitting on a garage forecourt outside a big grey town, stirring in three packets of sugar and eating Mars Bars.

To keep our energy up, Luke says.

Like they are troops anticipating battle.

They sleep in the car, winding the front seats down so they form an arch on to the back. Making a quilt out of jackets and coats. Holding hands across the gear stick, smoking cigarettes, looking out at the sky.

Luke says: heading for?

Anywhere.

Name somewhere.

Finding a map on the back seat. Opening a page at random, putting her finger on the page, turning on the flashlight.

Where are we heading for?

Lower Shaw, says Pia.

Sounds horrible.

Well you think of a better way of deciding.

What about Fareport?

Fareport?

Over the years, so many times they heard Marie say: I want to visit Fareport Said so many times Sam drove them all there one night, on the way back from some holiday, on the long late drive home. Rainy dirty port.

A place to head for.

For breakfast they have stale buns, for lunch hot dogs and hot chocolate. Then, after the roads and the noise and their eyes almost closing as the cars speed by like conveyor belt prizes, they sleep in a field yellow with sun. Wake up red-faced and stiff but warmed to their centres.

Warm in every pore, Luke says and he smiles because the tiny car leaks brown water, making everything damp.

They buy chips in newspaper packages and frizzles of battered fish, then spend their last five pounds on petrol. Pia steals a bottle of shampoo. Washes her hair in a stream.

No money left.

Luke is sitting in the car, legs spread out through the open doorway.

Last three cigarettes.

He leans over on to the backseat and rummages around under a pile of newspapers and clothing.

One cheese sandwich, he says, half a burger and a can of Coke.

In the shopping centre of a big grey town there is a woman with a heavy bag of shopping, purse dangling out of the corner of her coat, Pia knocks into her.

I'm sorry.

No problem.

The woman rests her bags on the pavement for a moment, picks them up again, walks away.

And Pia has her brown leather purse in her hand, bulging with receipts and scraps of paper.

Back at the car, they take the money and ditch the rest: credit cards, a letter, scraps of paper, a postcard.

Darling Emma we must meet – reading the private letter in the park under the trees.

Don't forget, scrawled in watery black ink on the back of the postcard.

Tuna, eggs, cheese – on the scrap of lined paper. Order milk, pay school trip fee.

Seventy-two pounds.

Pia buys a take-away. Owner smiling broadly at her as she hands over a twenty pound note.

Cold weather, he says.

Yes.

But at least the sun shone for a few hours this afternoon.

Yes, Pia says.

Do you live locally?

No. Passing through – Pia lies – with my parents. On the way – the words come easily now and with a sense of trying them out – telling him: to visit Auntie Esther, helping to look after our aged aunt.

Pia buys petrol and chocolate bars, cigarettes and a bottle of gin.

It would be good, she says, to have somewhere to sleep tonight.

A bed, says Luke, and food at a table.

In the next town, Luke steals two purses and Pia takes a wallet.

Shouldn't be so easy, he says laughing. Laughing. We're going to be all right. I told you. What did I say?

He likes to hear the words: you were right. You said it would all work out.

You of little faith, tickling her.

Feeling like it is all in his control.

Scanning the newspapers, no reports yet that a boy and his sister have gone missing. Wondering suddenly about Sam and Marie. What would they tell people? What could they say?

Fareport. Pia and Luke book into the Sea View guest house. They follow the landlady, her rump swaying almost gracefully up the narrow staircase. Winding round. Squeezing in shoulders and arms dangling as they jostle framed photographs and paintings already lopsided on the walls; fishing boats on calm seas and portraits of sailors with faces wrinkled like prunes.

This room has a sea view, she announces, opening the door wide.

A sea view and a quilted nylon bedspread, a Teas Maid and a family of china Dalmatians.

She leads them across the hall, lacy slip creeping down tan-stockinged legs.

This one is more expensive because it has its own bathroom.

She exhibits the olive-coloured bathroom suite, leaving the door ajar to allow a peek of crocheted toilet roll cover – a poodle on hind legs, extravagant pom-pom instead of a nose.

They take the room with the bathroom en suite. Pay for two nights in advance.

Is that all you will be staying?

Luke says: we don't know.

Visiting Auntie Esther, Pia says.

Later that evening, while the landlady plies them with chicken breast and gravy, Pia and Luke invent stories of their aunt's antics.

Do you remember the time her cat got stuck on the roof and they had to call the fire brigade? Luke says.

Yes, says Pia, they arrived with the sirens going.

But the cat would not go down the ladder with any of them, it was terrified and hissing and scratching. So Auntie Esther had to go up the ladder and bring her cat down.

One of the firemen threw the cat across the roof to her.

Oh yes, and she screamed and Uncle Hugh went running into the back garden to see if she had landed there.

Landlady smiling, smiling at them. Peach lipstick and a long rope of pearls around her scraggy neck.

Come in and say hello to George, she says, my husband.

Letting them step inside her plush red lounge.

George is in front of the fake log fire – brown plastic

logs and lurid flames. He offers Pia a whiskey, smiling gently.

To warm you up, he says, for the cold night.

Tall glass, dribble of dark liquid swirling around the bottom like a tidemark.

TV Times, a saucer of peanuts, a bowl of chocolates in individual pink foil packages. Pia wants one.

Here.

Pushing the bowl in front of her.

Have one, says George, and take another for later.

George looks as if the life has been pumped out of him, puff by puff, like the air out of a tyre. Stumpy hands laced tight in his lap. But as the landlady turns away, the man's false teeth jump out of his mouth – for a fraction of a moment Pia is sure she saw them and the eyes, without their veil, are shining, laughing.

We have our dinner late, the landlady is explaining. After all the guests.

Pia imagines reheated custard, cold greens and fruitless bits of pie. And George in a hand-knitted cardigan still looking at Pia.

Better be going, Luke says, standing in the doorway.

Out then into the hall, knocking against a shelf stacked with ornaments.

Mind the cow – the landlady catches it. Black and white china cow with udders and a tail.

It's precious to my wife, says George as they leave.

The sea at low tide. Pale slate bathed in a light that trembles. Long shadows along the beach. Alone except for the fishing boats, barnacled hulls creaking and the seagulls, swooping and rising.

Steps in the dark down the cliff path. There is a yellowish scum on the wet sand at their feet and beer bottles, tourist leaflets and moist animals crawling, tangled up in the stringy green. A broken flip-flop is in the net also and a small cluster of brittle shells, pearl tarred oily-black.

Emerging from the shadows, there is a pier between sand and sea, leading out. Almost tumbled down, a climbing frame of iron beams; weeping orange-brown scabs. Slimy with limpets and pulpy green moss.

Jumping down off the pier in the darkness, Pia feeling a strong wind pushing her along. Running arms out towards the sea, with the space melting over her, Pia opens her mouth and screams, screams to the sky and whatever else may be up there.

The next day, Pia is lifting a leather purse from a woman in a fur-collared coat and the woman turns and traps Pia's wrist under her fingers. Hand like a claw, purple-veined and bony. The woman drips face powder. Bright orange lips.

Got you. Little thief.

Claws hooking tighter.

Pia kicks her hard, in the shin, bites the woman's hand and as the woman lets go, Pia starts to run. Knocking over a trestle table of puppets carved out of wood, colliding with a child on a push bike, tripping on a kerb.

Pia says: I can't do it any more.

Yes you can, Luke says. You've got to. We've got to pay the landlady – or get more petrol. Need bus fare, he laughs – just to get to where we ditched the car.

Plastic windmills rattle outside kiosks stacked with inflatable animals and model boats, sticks of rainbow-coloured rock, sunglasses and straw hats. On the street there are racks of postcards: drawings of blonde women with melon-shaped breasts and oily-looking men with eyes and tongues on springs.

A young man is reading through them all rapaciously, eyes flicking quickly down the rows. When his friend comes out of the shop, the man stops looking and pretends he thinks the cards are stupid. He looks like the men on the postcards, thinks Pia, wet-mouthed and deceitful.

Bumping against jackets and coats, Pia is reaching into a bag, clamping her hand round a small oblong shape. Her wrist is caught in the bag strap and Pia is wrenching her hand away because she thinks she sees her, the woman with bright orange lips.

Pia looks up and the woman is gone.

Luke finds Pia on the steps of the library.

I can't do it, she says.

Grinding a cigarette butt into the white stone of the step.

He says: I'll steal for both of us. Says: it doesn't matter. You can hover, he says, watch me, be my extra pair of eyes.

Back on the street, Luke is confident too soon, losing his nerve at the final moment. So close to getting caught.

Running, both of them running away and Pia's heart bangs like someone is drumming on her breastbone.

Pia and Luke walk past the bingo halls and the penny arcades, the hot-dog stalls where burnt onions are sizzling; cockles and whelks, a mass of jelly eyes.

They sit on a bench on the seafront eating vanilla ice cream. The biggest cones the woman had and with a chocolate flake inserted and a fudge stick and, over it all, thick butterscotch sauce. Looking out towards the churning sea.

Liquid ice cream running down Pia's chin. Salty wind blowing. Strands of hair sticky with butterscotch whipping against her cheeks; wiping them away with sauce-sticky fingers. Ice cream on her cuff and creeping up towards her elbow. Ditching the cone at last, soggy with all the good bits melted to mush and watching a thin bird feasting, tar-heavy wings awkward at its sides.

glory

They miss one night's rent. The landlady's portion of chicken breast at dinner is more meagre.

When can I expect payment?

Tomorrow, Luke says.

And in the silence, the screech of his knife across the plate.

Pia and Luke empty their pockets on to the candlewick bedspread, root through old carrier bags. Cobble together ten pounds.

Tonight, he says. We've got to get the money tonight.

Spending the ten pounds on a bottle of whiskey.

Cool my nerves, he says, steady my hand.

But the whiskey makes him clumsy and his clumsiness makes him frustrated. He drinks more whiskey.

An old man comes out of the off-licence. Luke hesitates a moment too long, kicking a wall as the man crosses to the other side of the road.

A woman buys champagne in the off-licence and a bag of tortilla chips. The buckles on her shoes sparkle. She smells like the inside of a shop.

As she climbs into her blue BMW Luke curses her.

Old hag, he calls after her. Witch.

Luke's anger is a snake eating its own tail.

As it starts to rain, he turns on Pia.

It's your fault, he says. If you hadn't got caught then I wouldn't be feeling so nervous. You've jinxed us both. I'd be better off on my own.

Better off on my own.

Pia watches Luke stumble away into the evening.

She wants to run after him.

All her fault.

Back in the room waiting for Luke. Pia hears footsteps on the landing. Then a tap at the door.

May I come in?

George is whispering.

Pia unlocks the door. Lets the old man inside.

Are you all right?

Noticing that she has been crying, the crumpled state of the bedding, clothes all over the floor.

I'm fine.

Where's your brother?

Out.

Are you sure you're okay?

Bursting into tears, telling him: we have run out of money and we've got no one to help us and I don't know what to do.

Feeling his shirt button up against her cheek, his fat-fingered hand caught up in her hair.

Running, running away from George and the bedroom, out the front door of the guest house and across the empty street.

Stillness broken by the sound of cars. A street away, the pub spilling out. Voices and headlamps lighting up the street.

Hello darling.

A voice behind her.

Want a lift somewhere?

No.

Walking faster.

Are you sure? I know a good route – the man rolls the word out thick with innuendo and now she hears several of them laughing.

Pick a car, says one of them, any car.

Wanting to turn around and scream at them, walking faster, fast as she can.

You all right?

The man pulls up in a car beside her.

I saw you, he says, outside the pub back there. Wanted to check you were okay.

Thank you, yes.

Still walking.

Can I offer you a lift?

No.

It's late and dark, he says. You could get into trouble. Where are you going?

Going?

Stopping suddenly in the street.

Come with me, he says.

He has a flat with a view across the tops of trees. White leather seats. Flowers in a vase. He pours her a glass of wine. Watches as she walks across the lounge to look out of the smoked-glass window.

Name's Ryan, he says.

Pia.

What are you doing here?

What do you mean?

How do you make your living?

My living?

How much?

Much?

She looks at his thin grey mouth.

For the works, he says, you know what I mean.

Pia says: I don't do that.

Don't you? Looking at her from her shoes up her legs, her chest, her face.

Easy way to earn some money, he says, all you've got to do is lie on your back. How much?

No.

Fifty pounds, he says. Seventy-five?

With seventy-five pounds they could pay the landlady off and put petrol in the car.

Seventy-five pounds, he says, what do you say?

They could get the hell away from here and Luke would be happy with her again, not blaming her for the mess, not wanting to leave her behind.

He asks her to repeat it—

all right, she says, I said all right—

and then he starts to move across the carpet towards her.

The bedroom I think, he says, guiding her towards it.

Turning on the bedside lamp to see a woman's trinkets – a book, a pen and a ring.

Pia perches on the edge of the bed with her knees together, watches him take off his navy spotted tie, his blue striped suit.

The man says: don't you think you should take your clothes off?

And Pia starts slowly unbuttoning.

Yes, she says.

Do you mind if I call you Sarah?

No.

No?

I don't mind.

Pia closes her eyes against the rocking and the feel of him banging against her body, the knowing he is inside of her. *Inside.*

And just at the moment when she thinks she cannot take it, this is too much for me, get me away, he comes with a little cried fanfare and slumps against her belly.

Thank you, he says.

And taking off the rubber, folding it into a tissue, rearranging the clothes she has not taken off, Pia thinks: rent in my hand.

Luke likes the money. Likes her for getting the money. More than likes her, glories in her.

Fucking brilliant, he says.

His smile lighting them both up like a lamp.

Money makes him feel as if he is winning, like everything isn't stacked on the other side. Makes him walk different, makes him feel he has things to say.

Fucking brilliant, he says, tickling her on the mattress.

And she is laughing because he is laughing and because it is as if his happiness is directly linked to her own, as if they both feed off the same supply. Like when he doesn't get his fix, she doesn't get hers.

We can make plans, he says.

Watching him fizzing with them.

Paris, he says. Amsterdam. Rome.

Pia tells Luke: Gerard helped. In a strange way. In a strange, twisting let's try to make something good out of something awful way. It is like doing it with Gerard, she says, over and over.

But not as bad, she tells him. Never as bad.

after

Pia and Luke are gone. Why don't you go?

How long has Marie been storing up those words, nursing them like a baby, watching them grow fat on all she keeps hidden inside?

Why don't you? Why don't you go?

Following Sam up the stairs and into the bedroom where he starts packing a suitcase.

Her voice prods at him like a bony finger.

Sam is folding up a shirt, scrunched up balls of underpants and socks.

Who do you think will have you? What sort of life do you think you'll have?

And Marie is starting to hit him now. Fists banging against his body. She could have loved him. If he'd tried harder, been more kind. She didn't set out to ruin his life or to end up stuck with him in this slow, burning hate.

I could have loved him over time, she thinks, I could have got over Joe.

Joe. She can still smell his tobacco, some nights when she is out in the garden and a neighbour's bonfire or a cigarette perhaps pulls him back strongly to her.

He did not want her. Not in the end. Not with Pia. And he was her chance – she knows that now – to be happy.

I would have loved Pia, she thinks. As I loved Pia's father, instead of him, as a substitute. But Pia would not let me, Pia would not give me anything to love.

Go then, Marie says. Better off without any of you. From now on, she says, I shall do exactly – and she rolls out the word *exactly* like a red carpet for herself – exactly what I like.

Leaving, Sam thinks only: at last.

Outside the front door, outside on the street, outside. Does Sam only imagine that the air is cleaner? Only imagine that it makes a more direct route for his lungs and expands them to twice their usual size.

Breathing in the air and, with it, the sights, the sounds, the smells of an ordinary street. Ordinary people doing ordinary things. And he is one of them. Suddenly, miraculously. And all because Marie is on the other side of that door.

Why didn't he do it a hundred years ago?

Because I could not have left Pia, he thinks, but now Pia is gone.

Sam walks for a while. Unusual for him to be walking rather than driving. Unfamiliar the sensation of his moving legs and feet. But they seem to be moving him forward effortlessly, like they don't need a command, like they've been primed for ages and ready to go.

Primed for decades.

There were the years of loving Anna, he thinks, after the weeks of pushing Anna away. All those years of loving Anna and living in Marie's house. Anna wanted him to leave Marie. She said she'd walk away from it all. If he would. If he could.

I can't leave Pia, he told her.

We can take her with us.

But Sam never found the words to tell her: Pia is not mine to take.

Remembering when Pia was small she used to say she was from a foreign country. She spoke gobbledy gook. Made dramatic gesticulations with her hands. Pia and Sam would piece together an alphabet, a few words. Communication.

What is your country like?

It was her favourite question.

Sea.

Making waves with her arms and fingers.

Sun.

Feigning sunstroke.

Clear sky.

Open arms.

Hope she finds it. With all his heart, every part of it, wanting Pia to find her country.

Hope she finds it – like a prayer, the closest he's come to prayer in years. And feeling a tightness in his throat now. So much forgotten feeling.

And now a lightness. Incredible lightness. She will find her country and he will find her again. Free to walk and carry on walking. Matching his steps to the mantra of hope in his head.

Marie does not get up until midday. Spends the whole day in her dressing gown. Smoking cigarettes, watching daytime television, peering through the curtains at the neighbours to remind herself of life.

The entire house is her bed, trawling her duvet around with her wherever she goes. Alone, Marie leaves the washing-up in the sink, washing items only as she needs them: a teaspoon, a fork, wiping a quick cloth around a bowl. Eating only because she has to. Food tastes of cardboard and sits in her body like rocks.

A small bare room. A phonecall one night to Anna. Receiver sticky in the brown and beige bedroom. And the television in the corner, volume down but still it's blaring.

Hello?

Her voice.

Hello?

Again.

What to say to her?

Hello?

And the receiver is back on the hook and Sam is sweating. Sitting on the bed in his hotel room and trembling. Anna. All he had to say was Anna. She would have known it was him. She would have come. She would.

Anna comes.

    After the third call. On the fourth:

    Is that you Sam?

    Speaking into the silence.

    And then his own voice, sounding stronger than he imagined.

    Anna.

    Do you want to see me?

    So easy, always, she paves the way—

    Yes.

    And she comes with a bag. A long red and green chequered bag and it's heavy so she leaves it in the hall.

A new life. It is possible to have a new life, Sam thinks, waking next to Anna. His Anna. Said she was always.

    Shabby tweed and wood room but so early in the morning, alongside the drone of cars, the sound of birds. Closer than the cars. A wake-up-to-the-day chorus.

    Anna.

    Waking her.

    Did you always know that I would call you?

    Asking her.

    Rubbing her eyes.

    No, she says. Not always.

four pounds a minute

The first one paid over the odds. Pia learns that quickly. The next one will only pay twenty-five.

Take it, he says, or leave it.

He has a bristly face, grey eyes, a beaten up denim jacket.

The company car smells of lilac air-freshener. There is a child's red skateboard on the back seat, a half-eaten packet of Minstrels, a pair of navy woollen tights.

Squashed up between the window and the hand brake, legs apart, hands clutching at the head rest, the dashboard, a marmalade tuft of his hair.

Counting: ten minutes since he opened the car door and smoothed cracker crumbs off the seat beside him, eight minutes since he pulled up into the lay-by and started unzipping his flies. That means she is getting paid four pounds a minute.

Four pounds a minute.

Pia feels big as she folds the notes into her pocket, not small and shrinking, but swelling inside the car, pushing up against the windows and doors. A strange man is happy to pay four pounds a minute to be with a body she finds easy to leave behind.

Pia watches her metamorphosis in the mirror.

Armour of eye shadow, blusher, lipstick.

Camouflage of short black skirt, striped jumper, cropped blue coat.

And she watches her postures alter, her gestures, her mind.

Liam, Warwick, David, Colin, Roy.

Liam says: women – roses and romance – always wanting bouquets and the right words. Then they want you to put on a performance, be the big stud and produce multiple orgasms. Women like certain things in a certain way. There are times, Liam says, when I feel inadequate.

I don't want to be bothered, he says, doing things the way a girlfriend wants me to do them. I'd rather come and pay a girl like you, who needs the money. No hassle, says Liam, no involvement, no commitment.

Afterwards, Liam asks: do you enjoy it?

Enjoy it? Pia looks across at him.

Yes, he says, does it turn you on?

No, she says, it's a job.

Then: is it normal?

Normal?

Yes, normal, he says, average.

What?

You see a lot of them, Liam says, is mine a fair size?
Pia looks at his face, damp with sweat still and puffy.
A fair size?
Pia pauses as if to think, to measure, to compare. And Liam sits very still in the silence, hands between his knees.
Yes, Pia says slowly. I think it is.

Pia lets her body slip away from her, eyes tight closed. Only opening them again when the belly and thighs pressing down on her have lifted from her body.

David says: I'm no charming prince. When I go out the girls do not flock around me. I enjoy sex – if I didn't have money I wouldn't have sex. I'm privileged. You pay for many privileges in life.
David says: I'll give you extra money if you kiss me.
But Pia says: I don't do that.
Because kissing is intimate. Because she has to keep something of herself for herself.

Pia pretends the man is not there, puts up a glass wall. Thinks about the money, what she and Luke can buy with it, thinks about the place in the sun they want to get to.

Roy asks: why are you doing this? Can't you find a nice man to keep you?
And Roy asks: what's on your mind?

And Pia tells him the truth because she feels like it.

I hope the condom doesn't break, she says, I hope you pay, she says, and I hope to hell you hurry up.

Back at the guest house, Pia washes her face and arms and thighs. Every part of her body, taking care not to miss an inch, going over it. Over and over.

fisherman

Pia wants her father.

Calls Sam in the middle of the night, just to hear his voice.

Marie answers the telephone: yes?

And then into the silence, she says: yes again, and: who is there?

And Pia hangs up the telephone. Can't talk to Marie – not even to say hello.

Pia tries calling the next night, and the next. Always Marie's voice.

At last Marie says: is that you Pia?

And she says: I want to talk to Sam.

Sam?

Marie laughs. Pia hears the clink of bottle against glass.

Have you been drinking?

Yes, drinking, says Marie. Lots of drinking.

Where's Sam?

Sam doesn't live here any more.

He's gone?

That's right, says Marie. He's run away.

Do you know where he is?

Run away like you. Left me on my own.

Do you have his telephone number?

No, says Marie. And then: I doubt he'll try to find you.

Pia says: you don't know that.

Yes, Marie says, I do.

She wants to wipe it all away like a chalk smudge on a blackboard, wants to draw in something new, something with more beautiful lines, saying:

Sam is not your father.

Not my father?

Pia feels her knees like water.

Your father was a fisherman, Marie says. He didn't want you. Said he wasn't good with children – Marie remembering – said they drove him – she can hear his voice – they drove him insane.

He didn't want you and so he didn't want me. He was my chance to be happy.

Happy – the word reverberates around the telephone box. And you ruined it.

Pia is running from the payphone and across the street. Past the burger bar, the alleyway next to the chip shop and the derelict car on waste ground. Through the woods, past the lightning-struck tree, the railway station car park and the back of the supermarket where the lost trolleys are found.

When Luke finally finds Pia she is sitting under one of the sinks in the ladies' toilet.

Fisherman.
For a while that is all she can say.

Pia dreams of her father, the fisherman. He is sitting on the bank of a river with a line in his hands and a jar on the grass beside him. There are maggots in the glass, plump on children's blood and he is picking them out of the jar, one by one, and forcing a metal hook through their bodies.

Pia wakes tangled up in sheets.

Pia dreams of her father, the fisherman. He goes out to sea with a rowing boat and a net. Scoops up oceans full of rainbow-coloured fish. They fall tinkling on to the wooden base of the boat, slipping over his boots and he squashes them with every movement he makes. A boat filled with fish gills and fish stomachs and fish hearts.

Pia dreams of her father, the fisherman. He is the head of a fleet of gleaming boats. White cap, shirt, shoes and trousers. Glistening on the deck of a ship riding into the sun. Standing on the harbour, Pia is calling out to him. But he is waving to someone behind her. When Pia turns to see who it is, it is a girl with Chloe's white hair.

chasing blues

A lorry driver, a travelling salesman, a solicitor, an accountant, a merchant seaman, two members of the armed forces,
an accountant with a false leg.

Money in our pockets, Luke says, to burn.

How happy he looks, standing in the bathroom in his
underpants, chin half-lathered with foam, smelling of tooth-
paste and deodorant and newly-washed hair. Hopping he is,
from one foot to the other—

Night on the tiles—

like a demented bird.

Chase your blues, he says, chase them away.

Landlady smiling, smiling at them again as they come down
the stairs shiny as new coins.

Lovely, she says. Lovely, because now the girl is working
the rent always comes in on time.

Luke's arm round Pia in the back of the taxi, smelling rose
air-freshener and damp coats.

No smoking in here.

The driver raps on the partition window.

Seven pounds fifty.

Holding out his hand.

Pia gives him a ten pound note.

Keep the change, she says.

Fish and pastries and dark red wine, lemon ice between courses, glasses the size of plates.

Pia and Luke drink champagne and grass-green liqueurs, bite thin mint sticks.

Passing food with their hands.

Eating slowly, very slowly. Chewing every morsel, keeping it in their mouths for a long time before swallowing. Mouths filled with delicious tastes.

The man is waiting for them by the door of the restaurant. As Pia gives a woman in black her cloakroom ticket, he steps forward and takes her hand.

I've been watching you both all evening. If you don't have any plans, why don't you come home with me?

He is tanned and gentle-eyed. Crocodile shoes. Gold watch. Plastic concertina of credit cards.

Following him outside, smiling with drink and excitement. Then huddled behind him in the back of the taxi.

Nothing to lose, says Luke.

Everything, says the man, to gain.

Their first cold rush of cocaine.

He divides the white powder up into three equal lines, sitting by the smoked glass coffee table, sipping Schnapps.

Here.

Turning to Pia, passing her a ten pound note rolled into a tube and breathing its cold white rush into her body.

Wanting to talk to him now and liking him, the way he swaggers round the penthouse, the sharp view out into the night.

Luke is sitting with his back pressed against Pia's legs. He is talking about car racing and betting on horses and the garden at their parents' house and the shed where he kept his bike.

So you have known each other for a long time?

Man's moon-shaped face, bubbling in front of Pia, like plastic burning.

We grew up together, Luke is laughing. Didn't we Pia?

She is nodding, praying: don't say brother and sister. Suddenly sober, then the room fizzes again.

Pia and Luke stay all night and all the next day. Roberto rolls spliffs on hardback books. Sprawling on a wine-coloured sofa, drinking sweet black coffee, eating strange packets of foreign biscuits.

The bathroom is white-tiled; steel sink, towels thick as velvet and as soft.

Pia asks: can I have a bath?

Help yourself. Calling out to her from the lounge.

Emptying a phial under the running water, dark yellow bubbles (and a smell she describes to Luke later as: rich).

Lying back in the wet heat, peering through the steam at the carved gilt-framed mirrors and Chinese spice jars, the rugs in purples, the coloured soaps.

Wanting this always.

I want this always.

Luke is sitting on the edge of the bath, a glass of champagne in one hand, a wobbly slice of gateau in the other.

Me, too.

Money.

Yes.

Taxis.

Yes.

Beautiful things.

Yes.

And the feeling, he says. Feels like nothing matters.

It is the first time, he is sure, he has felt this way. That nothing matters.

That feeling has got to be worth anything, he says.

Pia smiles at him, enjoying him.

Yes, she says, anything.

It seems to her as if she is making a pact with him tonight. Seeing him sitting on the edge of the bath, cream and jam around his mouth and purple shadows clear under his eyes because it is his second night without sleep and the rest of his face is very white. A pact that she will always, somehow, ensure that he can feel this happy, this forgetful.

Shouting from the lounge into the bathroom, Roberto says: I'm going to call Lilly. You've been gone ages, he says. Ages and ages. We need more entertainment, something different in here.

Lilly. Thigh high boots and red mesh tights. Black-rooted blonde, full make-up at dawn.

Roberto introducing her to Pia and Luke, one hand glued to her bottom.

H, Lilly calls it, Horse, Smack.

Unwrapping it in front of them.

Do you want some?

Heroin? Pia checks.

What else?

Pia shakes her head. Walks across the carpet towards Luke, puts her arm round him, whispers into his ear.

We don't need it.

He shrugs her off. Aren't you curious?

No. It's dangerous.

Eyes shining. Exactly, Luke says.

Dropper, syringe, spoon.

Watching Lilly suck water from a bowl. She mixes the white powder in the spoon and lights a match under it. She is filling a needle, searching for a vein, pressing, squeezing.

Done it before son?

Roberto moves away from Lilly, smiling.

Sure, says Luke, many times.

Luke holds the needle out to Pia – go on, why not? Go on, go on – right up to the last minute.

Pia shakes her head.

Watching Luke go there without her.

Wandering round Roberto's big rooms, bare toes on carpet, running her fingers along warm radiators.

Cupboards filled with tins of salmon and sweetcorn, asparagus and condensed milk. Opening tins of peaches, sitting on the table, pouring a river of cream into a bowl. Feet resting on a rosewood chair.

It is like being left behind on a railway platform, Pia thinks, with all your friends and your trunk on the train.

Pia watches a gameshow on the television.

This is my wife Rayna, says a man, and our son Marcus and our daughter Jude.

No, I don't like school, except for playing football – Marcus is red-faced and spotty.

He teases me, says his sister, behind our parents' back.

Grey-haired compere wags his finger.

Normal, normal, normal family smiling at the camera and answering questions. Laughing at the compere's jokes and thinking about the new car, the holiday in the sun, the pine fitted-kitchen and the gold-plated sink with taps.

Normal, normal, normal.

Let's hope – and the audience do – that this lovely family wins our star prize tonight.

Pia hears the telephone and rises from her chair, standing in the doorway, one eye still on the television.

Hello.

Get Roberto for me. Tell him it's Mike. And be quick.

He can't get to the phone right now.

Tell him it's urgent.

It doesn't matter how urgent. He's—

Tell him to call me.

Yes.

What's your name?

Chloe, Pia lies.

The city is lighting up: street lights, car headlamps, lamps lighting up rooms. Pia wants to go back to the guest house but Luke will not wake up. Listening to Roberto and Lilly. Talk of who cracked this one, chased that one, burgled that place. Talk of a painting, an eleven-carat diamond, forged hundred-dollar bills.

Roberto speaks on the telephone, holding conversations with Pia and Luke at the same time.

Roberto never mentions the word money, but he is always speaking about it.

Deals, he calls them. Favours.

No, he says into the receiver. Yes. Well done.

Roberto wants them to take a parcel from one side of town to the other.

Chance to make some real money, he says.

Easy money, Lilly says. When I met Roberto I was behind with bills. I owed money on my furniture, TV, HP, she says. Did a few deliveries. Cleared my debts off in a month. I needed a car, worked non-stop for a week and bought one. I needed a flat, worked two days and rented a good one. I wanted clothes, a video, satellite TV. Sent my son to boarding school where he can get the best.

A paper package wedged into Pia's rucksack between her diary and a sweatshirt.

Pia and Luke crossing town on a bus, reading aloud to each other from a newspaper:

A woman has been clubbed to death in a fight with her next-door neighbour.

A boy of six rescued his cat from a tree.

They have a cappuccino, sitting in a café, waiting for a woman with peroxided clipped hair and ounces of dark brown make-up. They watch her as she drinks tea and eats a doughnut.

When she leaves, they follow her. Through the busy streets and round corners. Past a baggy line of teenagers jittery in the cold. Through swing doors and up a staircase, graffiti spidering the walls. A pile of puke in a corner. Crumpled newspapers and cigarette butts.

Along a corridor where a boy is sucking water out of a tap.

Sizzling head, he says. Hot, dry.

Into a dark room, then another filled with smoke.

The woman puts the package in a drawer beside the bed. Pia sees cigarettes, coins, odd earrings and scraps of paper.

Kohl in thick rims around her eyes.

Well done, says Roberto and he pays them – part cash, part plastic bag of Thai grass.

One eighth of human beings own seven-eighths of the social cake for no better reason than accident of birth. All those mugs, Roberto says, going to work, he says, going home, kissing the wife, kissing the kids, going to bed. Getting up, he says, and doing it all over. Idiots, he says. Docile idiots. Life drained out of them, conforming out of fear.

The next package goes to a woman in a kitchen. Chip fat hangs in the air, two children at a table, fighting.

Stop it you two.

Turning, shouting.

Taking the package from Pia and tucking it in the front pocket of her jeans.

Wait a minute, will you?

The woman walks out of the room and is gone so long Pia snatches a chip from one of the boy's plates, pops it lukewarm into her mouth.

The woman is pink in the face, hair straggling around her head.

Not enough, she says looking up at them then back at her leather purse. I haven't got enough.

Pia shrugs. What to do?

Tell him, says the woman, I will give him the rest next time.

One hand on the package in her pocket, she looks as if she is collapsing in on herself. Walking them to the door, she does not step outside.

Coke to keep them going, marijuana to chill them out, and Temazipan, Roberto says, to send them to sleep.

Roberto takes Pia into a back bedroom, opens a wardrobe filled with dresses, says:

Choose yourself a gift from me. Something frivolous, he says, an indulgence. When you have found what you like, show it to me

Twirling in front of him in a black dress made up of strings of beads.

A million dollars, he says. A princess.

You like the work, Roberto says, making coffee for them in his kitchen. I knew you would, he says, it is easy. It's your one chance to make big money. Just keep your head clear, he says, and your loyalties strong.

Pia likes the lifestyle.

The new clothes, she says, and the presents. Paying the landlady in advance, not feeling like meat.

Luke likes the H. Likes the lightness, says: I'm flying. Like lightness is the only thing that matters, floating off from everything he knows.

Luke says: I don't need it, it's a choice. I just like it, he says. LIKE IT. It is because you believe the hype, that's why you're afraid.

Luke says: it makes it easier to function. Luke says: being straight makes me itchy if I do it for too long.

A wiry man, woolly hat worn against the first chill of autumn.

Pia and Luke count the money in a back lane – five thousand pounds in a tight wad, and their share is only seventy-five.

Roberto is ripping us off, Luke says.

It's his connections, says Pia, his deals.

Pia is walking away, heading for the bus stop, when Luke runs up behind her, grabs her by the arms and spins her around.

Let's lose a deal, he says.

What?

Pretend we got mugged, he says, and keep the money for ourselves.

Pia says: I don't want to get into this any deeper. Let's just do the work and get away.

But Luke says: I'm on a roll, I can feel it. Let's keep it for ourselves. Just once. Stock up our balance.

Pia tries to walk on but Luke will not let go of her.

This could be it, he says. You and me in clover. The more money we make, he says, the sooner we can be out of here.

And go where? says Pia.

Somewhere where the sun shines.

Where the sun shines.

Pia has a picture in her head from a travel brochure.

Turquoise sea, she tells him, miles of white sand and the sun in a huge clear sky. You and me in a hotel, she says, room service, a balcony under the stars.

All of that, yes, says Luke. And more.

———

Luke tells Roberto: we were mugged.

Coming back through the park, he says, we stopped to buy an ice cream. A big man behind me in the queue. He must have had a knife with him. He cut the ruck-sack clean off my shoulders. He was gone in the instant I turned around, sprinting across the green, I ran after him – didn't I Pia?

Pia nods her head.

Ran and ran, didn't we Pia?

Yes. But he was too fast.

He jumped into a car, says Luke.

What sort of car?

A Citroën.

What colour?

Black – the lies coming thick and fast and so easy, thinks

Luke because he can see it all in his head as he is speaking. It should not be this easy to get five thousand pounds.

But now Roberto is twisting Pia's arm behind her back and Luke is saying:

it's the truth, honest. Honest. We're not lying.

Roberto sees Pia standing there, looking up at him, a look he cannot interpret in her eyes.

It's the feeling of being cheated, he says, one hand punching into the other. Makes me into a madman, he says, but no excuse for beating up on a little girl.

That night, leaving Roberto's flat, Pia and Luke are jumped on. Three men straddle Luke's body and hit him around the head. They rip his clothes, empty his pockets, stub out their cigarettes on his legs.

When Pia and Luke stagger back to Roberto's flat, Lilly speaks to them through the intercom.

We're in trouble, Pia says.

Roberto doesn't want to see you. Not tonight, says Lilly, not ever again.

lavender

Luke wakes tangled in the rug on the floor, reaches for his tobacco tin, his lighter, his leather pouch of hash. Rolls a joint shakily but quickly, draws the smoke deep into his lungs. Sees Pia curled around the leg of the armchair. The faded blue armchair with patched-up arms, like a rag doll, thinks Luke, a fat blue rag doll.

He wishes he did not ache so much; his gums, his teeth, his jaw. Shooting pains in his arms, stinging cramp in his feet. Pia is sleeping peacefully. One arm slung out above her head. It's as if she carries their troubles through the day, he thinks, then passes them to him at night.

He wishes he could stop thinking. All these thoughts and no answer to anything. It's the trying-to-make-sense-of, that's why he needs it – the honey-gold release, the feeling of it all dropping away.

Reaching for Pia now, reaching into her sleep and pulling her out.

He thinks: if I can find the right words to describe it to her she will understand.

He says: you don't have to be miserable, struggling with the mess, feeling useless and small. You can fly, he says. Fly.

And it's not that she's not tempted, not that he doesn't make it sound wonderful and near. It's because she knows she'll like it, like he does, more than anything and then—

No, she says pushing the polythene bag away.

As long as he has enough H, they are
sailing, he says.
Head in her lap and sailing.
She is on the shore trying to reach him, wanting to pull him out.
Swim with me.
Wanting her with him.
I'm only inches away, she says.

Luke trying to stop.
Luke not trying to stop.
Every other hour shouting. SHOUTING. Punching walls, cowering, crying.

And no money again.

Lavender legs in stilettoes. Lycra mini. Floral blouse.
A street lamp splashes orange in the puddles. A car with yellow headlights. A man. A smeary window.
Hello love.
Pia teeters over.

Brown eyes. Dry lips.

Cold night, he says.

Yes, she says.

She takes him into a room in a derelict flat: a single bed with a sheet, a makeshift wardrobe, curtains, armchair, dim light.

Light on, she says, or off?

On

(highlighting makeup, bottles of Cinzano, a half-eaten burger smothered in red chilli sauce).

Off, he says. Off.

He is standing in front of her breathing. All she can hear is his breathing and the sound of her own heart. It hurts when it bangs, likes she's been running and running.

Come here, he says.

He puts a rough hand inside her blouse. Pulls a breast free and moulds it between his fingers.

Nipples like stones. And the rest of her, stiff as parchment, all angles and sharp lines. Ice fingers moving too hard and then not hard enough so that he wants to shout at her. SHOUT. What-the-bloody-hell-do-you-think-I'm-paying-you-for?

He comes too quickly in that one fatal instant when his mind is somewhere else.

Twenty pounds.

He uncreases two ten pound notes, arranges them on the wooden dresser.

In the mirror, he sees her, hair falling in a red tangle in front of her face.

How old are you?
Why?
Friendly question, he says.
Don't need it, she says.

———————

Luke is in a filthy mood. Like he's been standing under clouds all day. Pia can barely see him for cigarette smoke.

How many tonight? he asks.

Six.

His palm is against her cheek, so soft, the sensation travels through her body.

One hundred and fifty pounds.

The notes crackle between his fingers.

They eat sandwiches and chocolate. Picking candle wax off the landlady's window-sill, knee to knee.

She looks tired and he wants to take that look away. He turns on the radio. The boom boom boom of a drum making everything jump slightly.

Come here Pia, he says. Pia, he says – and she is walking towards him, fingers touching his fingers, being pulled on to his lap where she can rest for a while, head against his head, the warm feeling of his legs along the back of hers. He smells of streets and apple shampoo.

I don't want to work tonight, whispering it into his hair.

I know, he says.

They go to see a movie. Eat chocolate toffees in the darkness, hold hands.

She does not believe in happy endings, even though the couple look happy at the end, standing on the deck of a ship, looking out at the sea. She knows it won't last, not that happiness. It's like the first time she saw a freesia, or stayed up past midnight or won at cards. Like a washing-up-liquid bubble. A shimmer of colour and then *pop*.

Outside on the street, Luke ruffles Pia's hair. It feels gritty between his fingers. Gritty and soft, winding it through and around, like a thread. He wants to hold her, here, right here on the street with the grey people watching and the lights rained hazy.

But she is sad tonight. Always sad.

You haven't learned to forget. He's always telling her. You carry everything around with you. Put it down – half shaking half stroking her – put it down.

He keeps their money in an ice-cream carton on top of a pile of books. Creased dirty notes in an elastic band. Counts them: one hundred, two hundred, twenty, forty, sixty. If she said: give me some, he would peel a few notes away from the others, give them to her. Our money. He calls it: our money. But he is in charge of it.

Not long now, he keeps saying – turquoise sea, long white sands.

As if time means anything, thinks Pia. As if an hour can't feel like a day.

She plugs in the kettle, while he counts their money. He takes his jacket off to do this, switches on the table light.

He regrets taking her to the movies. She can feel it. It's money he could be feeling between his fingers and counting. He wishes she had gone to work.

There is a bottle of red wine under the bed. They have been saving it for a special occasion, but tonight he opens it without asking her, downs a glass before he pours one for her, holding on tight to the bottle so that his fingers pinch white.

Don't, she says.

What?

It's the way she says it, like she's frightened of him. He stands, shaking her off although she is not touching him, just the shadow of her, the imprint. She feels like a second skin sometimes, wrapping round him too tight.

Don't go out.

Why not?

She is looking at the ground – the money.

What?

Last time he got mad, he blew the lot. Twenty ten pound bags. They had to start from scratch then. Filling the tin back up. Ten men. One day she'd had ten men and then he spent the whole lot at once.

It is because she is doing it for him, he says. He feels like he owes her and that makes him angry. So angry he wants to throw her against the wall and watch her smash like a melon. She is doing it for him and sometimes it makes him hate her.

He wants her to smoke a bag with him. Says it will make her forget. Says once she has forgotten she will feel better.

Better than you can imagine, he says. It's like flying without leaving the room.

He wants them to smoke a bag together. Says it will make them closer, says if she understands he won't get so angry, won't need to.

She says she doesn't understand and she doesn't want to.

I want to get away from here, she says. Properly away. Not just in my head.

There is a boy walking along the street towards her. He is wearing a denim jacket with badges sewn to the sleeves. His shoelaces are undone. He is trying not to look at her but he can't help it, peering up and out from under a long fringe.

Hello, Pia says.

But he does not answer.

A girl with a pram, bumping up the kerb and her baby starts crying. Squawking and wailing. She looks harassed. Standing on the corner, jiggling the pram and making soft angry noises. Last straggly stages of a perm. Fake-fur coat. She catches Pia staring and glowers at her.

A day to be at home. A day when Pia's belly button feels as if it is outside of her clothes and it is pulling bad things into her.

There is no hole in your belly – Luke is always telling her. You're as sealed up as I am. Nothing can get in unless you want it to.

He only thinks that because he is a boy. If he had her body he'd know. Then he'd know.

Got a light?

The man is wearing a long coat. Long hair, frothy beard.

She pulls a lighter from her pocket, hands it to him.

How much?

She wants to says: a fiver for the lighter. She says: Twenty-five pounds.

Twenty-five pounds, he says, for a fuck. No way. Too much.

She wants to say: fuck you, FUCK YOU. FUCK OFF. She says: twenty but no lower.

Fifteen.

FUCK OFF.

Pia sees Luke across the street, in a doorway, he is looking at her and smoking, surrounding himself with smoke. She shrugs her shoulders, mouths: *moron*, indicating the man just leaving. Luke looks away.

The next one doesn't care about money. Wants to pay extra for extra things.

Like what?

No rubber. He whispers it into the air by her neck. Ten pounds more, he says.

No way.

Fifteen.

No.

Twenty-five.

Pia thinks of the money.

I don't do that, she says.

A man who just wants to hold her in his car. On the front seat.

Fifteen minutes, he says, that's all I need. So when my ex walks home from work she can see us.

So she sits with him in his car and watches him fiddle with his car radio until one minute to four when he pulls her across the gear stick towards him and sticks his tongue in her ear.

Eyes bolt open, Pia sees the woman as she pulls open the car door behind him, grabs him by the hair, starts pulling him to the ground.

Pia holds tight to the money he gave her. Steps out of the car and walks away.

Straight sex. Oral sex. Hand jobs. Blow jobs. Letting them dress in women's clothes. Domination. Prostitute as counsellor, as listener, as girlfriend, as friend.

Pia can leave her body behind like a glove, loose and empty

on the pavement. She can be a cloud, a breath, a whisper, so it doesn't matter.

That's what she tells Luke: it doesn't matter what they want, as long as it doesn't hurt.

But it does matter.

Sometimes, now, when Luke is inside of her, it is not his face she sees, not his face when she looks up into his grey-green eyes, but a blurry-faced stranger who is calling her: Diane. Or: Sophie. Or: mother. It matters.

Pia.

It is eleven o'clock in the morning and Luke is shaking her gently.

Time to get up.

Opening the curtains wide.

Below, the bustle of the street, umbrellas and car hooters, shoes on pavements, the screeching of brakes.

A woman calls out: you'll be sorry. Wait and see, she yells, your life won't be so great without me.

Half-sleeping, struggling to be awake, Pia imagines the woman standing on the pavement and the man walking away from her; no, he's running. Running. Pia imagines him crawling back a week later, maybe two, trying not to know the woman was right: there are no great things out there, only more, Pia thinks, of the same.

Pia.

Yes.

It's time to get up.

Luke is red-eyed, itchy. Springing around the room, colliding with walls and doors. The room is too small for him again. She can feel it. He is full of punching energy. Needing to explore.

Got to get out, he says.

Out on the streets in the light. Sunglasses on, coat collar pulled up and around his neck and ears.

It's cold, he says.

Yes.

Got to get some tea.

The café windows are white with steam. Gingham table cloths, handprints on the walls. He orders eggs and coffee and toast. He likes to look at the chipped blue china plates and the wobbly piles of food and the grease sitting like a skin on everything.

Pia spreads jam on a slice of toast, eats quickly. She can hear him tapping one foot against the other. Darting eyes. Like he's being hunted. Or there's something he's got to find.

Ready?

She is drinking tea, tracing its course down her throat into her belly.

Hurry.

She drinks quickly, stubs her cigarette out in the green plastic ashtray.

He is out of the door and she is following him.

In the park, he throws stones in to the pond, not aiming for the ducks and red-beaked geese, not really, but not minding when they squawk and splash, liking the sudden beating of their wings.

There is a boy with a toy boat.

Looks like he's got lots more at home, Pia says. Drawers and cupboards crammed with things to please him. Anxious, smiling parents.

I'm going.

She wants to say: don't, but she knows it will make him angry and then he will leave, leave to spite her and it will all end up being her fault.

Where?

You know where.

Please don't.

He is walking away.

Let me come with you.

Walking away.

Waiting for him now is not so different, thinks Pia, to when I was fourteen. Not so. Loving him feels the same. The same hurting. The same hating. And no one to tell.

What would the girls have said? Sucking on their cigarettes, handing each other chewing gum and lip balm and an apple that kept going around.

Your brother. You're in love with your brother.

Forming a wall against her.

Alone in the guest house, waiting for him to come because he is the only one she can talk to. He always was.

Pia goes out on to the street because the clock won't lie or jump around or make time disappear.

She goes out on to the street because the room is getting smaller or she is getting bigger and she will surely be crushed.

Feeling the cold in her toes.

Pia stamps her feet to try to warm them. Four fifteen. Luke could be anywhere. Watching the street. Anywhere at all.

Tom is a regular. Six foot six, shoes like surf boards, rough hands and eyes to match. But gentle. Likes to talk first. Whispering into the darkness. Likes to use Pia's name, tell her about his week.

Makes it more personal.

Personal.

Like you're not a stranger – a total stranger. No more than a woman I could meet in the pub.

But he doesn't meet them in the pub.

Not often, he says.

Maybe never. Finds it hard to get beyond eye contact. Fleeting glances, he can hold them all right, return them, but then what? *Then what?*

Too many choices and his face reddens like a tomato while the woman looks away.

Tom's first time was with a prostitute. A woman his mother set him up with. He worried about her reporting back to his mother, pictured them at the kitchen table, sharing details, suggestions. But the woman made him feel on fire and there, really there with her in the room.

The second time was with a prostitute. Younger, prettier. He thought he was in love. He told her he was in love and he wanted her to be with him always. She gave up work, he saved. She made him happy, he says, in anticipation. One day she drew all the money out of their bank account and boarded an aeroplane.

She still sends him postcards, he says. Photos of beaches and markets. Lots of love, she writes, and kisses. He doesn't blame her, he says, not really. Thinks she'll be coming back.

Wants Pia to call him: lovely pumpkin. Comes quickly to that sound, quickly and with a shiver like pain.

Whenever he can afford to, he pays extra. An extra couple of pounds in the pile or in her hand at the door.

Back in the room, waiting for Luke. Same clock. Same walls. Same radio blaring weather reports and intimate family details: my son picks pockets, my daughter won't eat meals.

And the doctor advising: love your wayward children, love and help them whatever they do.

Six weeks of Luke saying: no more. I'm giving up. I'll stop.

Six weeks of clients and counting (minutes, pounds, hours).
Six weeks of watching Luke sink and fly, sink and fly.

One night, she found him hanging upside down on a bridge,
feet wedged through the railing, fingertips reaching down
to the sea. He said he was walking on the sky. Took her ten
minutes to talk him round and all the time she was holding
on to his scuffed, brown leather shoes.

Another night, he set fire to his coat. Flames licking all
around him and she could hear him laughing. Laughing, as
she threw a bucket of water over him. Sitting in a puddle
in black charred rags and laughing. Nothing matters when
you're flying, he says. That's the beauty of it that she can't see.
Nothing matters at all.

Pia packs a small bag and tries to write Luke a note. Ends up
writing him a letter which he will rubbish anyway, she knows,
believing it is all inside her own head. But she puts the letter
in a brown envelope and props it against the kettle where he
can't fail to see it because he drinks tea first, always, to make
him feel he's come into a room.

She takes down the ice-cream carton from the pile of books.
She doesn't count the money because she does not want to
know, not how much she is taking or how much she is
leaving behind. She divides the pile, roughly, in two, stashes
the money in the pockets of her jeans.

It is hard walking out, hard to decide and keep on deciding

that he is not good for her, not good, even though he is closer to her than the air.

Hard not to think of him being here without her.

Hard to keep putting one foot down in front of the other and doing it again. And again.

She feeds her key back through the letter box. Hears it clink against the stone step. Peering into the landlady's hall one last time. Smells of wood polish and air-freshener. Night air cold against her cheeks.

Need a hand with those?

Tom is leaning on the gate post, watching her position her bags.

No, she says, thank you.

Walking past him and away. But he is following her, following so close she can hear the clack of his shoes on the pavement.

Let me help you.

Walking alongside her.

She walks faster. He keeps pace.

Hovering around her at the bus stop, a tired moth with a singed wing.

Leave me alone, she says.

Only chatting.

Costs money, Pia says, to chat.

No bus and Pia's fingers are numbing.

Pia drinks tea in the café. Thick with sugar. Leaves in the

shape of hearts at the bottom of her cup. Hearts, she thinks, or ugly heads.

Fifteen-stone, bearded waitress sitting by a huge chrome teapot. An assortment of fruit and Madeira cakes in Cellophane, loaves of bread, eggs and sausages piled beside a double gas ring.

When Luke comes into the café, he sits opposite Pia at the table. He sees her bag but says nothing, leaning back in his vinyl chair, smoking a cigarette, making a sugar mountain out of a handful of grains.

Luke watches Pia eat a Chelsea bun, trailing sugar dust on her lips and the front strands of her hair.

Good? he says.

Good.

But she will not look at him, wiping the corners of her mouth with a serviette, licking sugar-gritty lips.

Another cigarette. Another small white mountain.

The jukebox with a cracked glass dome belts out Elvis Presley

Pia sees Luke, hunching forward in his denim jacket, studying the stained cloth. Sees his hands, his hair, his eyes. Sees the glass wall between them.

I'll give it up, he says at last. I will stop.

Not looking at Pia but at a tomato splodge on the tablecloth like a dried button of blood.

We'll save and go away, he says. Somewhere in the sun. I promise.

The sky is navy-blue and punctured with stars. Pia wishes she could rip it all away, like a backdrop at the theatre, paint on new colours, a day scene instead of night. Wishes she hadn't seen Luke's eyes, in the café, hadn't let him see hers.

Walking back is like knowing which horse is going to lose the race and betting on it anyway, she thinks. Walking back is easier than walking away.

Hurrying, running, under the dark arched sky, now that she can see the landlady's house and the lights are on and she can imagine Luke there, waiting for her. Imagine the candles burning and a bottle of wine. She can imagine him facing her as she walks in, smells of damp wood and apples and cigarette smoke.

He is flying. Stepping through the open door, she can see it straight away. Eyes like match heads, little dancing fires. He can't walk straight or sit in a chair, slipping all over the lounge on liquid limbs. But he is happy. She can see that too. By the curve of his mouth, the snake-like movement of his arms, the empty plastic packet on the table by the wall. Pia moves a cup out of his way, finds him a pillow for his head. Lies down beside him on the floor, on the thin and rumpled rug.

being saved

The first time Joe sees Pia, standing in the lay-by – cropped coat, red shoes scuffed at the edges and her long legs, long long legs – and her haireyesface, he feels a

– longing—

He finds the word only later. The word for the tingling, burning, empty-as-a-bush-after-a-fire feeling he has when he first looks at her. He wants to touch her.

One hundred pounds.

Touch her like a collector: slow, methodical. Or eat her, every last piece of skin and hair of her.

One hundred pounds?

She is trying it on. Joe sees rough red patches on her knees and elbows, chipped glitter polish on her nails. She needs a hot bath and a gallon of shampoo.

All right?

All right.

Because he wants to touch her tangled hair, the rough skin at her elbow, the—

Follow me.

She is leading him deeper into the alleyway. He is watching the back of her feet on high heels, wobbling. Silver shoulder-bag swinging. A small cut on the back of one leg, a ladder in her stocking.

Up a rickety metal stairway.

Joe catches sight of a boy skulking like a stray cat in the doorway. Sullen eyes. Mouth continually twitching. Smoking a cigarette, close to the butt. Dirty fingers that are on the verge of burning.

Up the stairs and they clank.

She unlocks the door to a derelict flat with the key round her neck. Turns on a small table light, turns to face him. Mascara in rings round her eyes.

Money first, she says.

And he is counting the notes into her hand: twenty, forty, fifty.

The girl is looking simultaneously at and through him.

At and through as if he is and isn't there.

Saying his name out loud to her: Joe

to give himself substance.

There is a strange yellow light in the room colouring everything.

What's your name?

I don't give my name, she says.

A way of staying private?

Of locking the important things inside. Of staying separate.

She says: you just bought half an hour.

She bends down to unbuckle her shoes. Tugs at the mesh curtain.

Light on, she asks him, or off?

There are clothes littered across the floor and the armchair, envelopes, biscuit-wrappers, glasses and ashtrays. Creased sheet on the bed, a dented heap of pillows.

On.

She is very thin. Hips jutting out like shelves. The grey sticks of her ribs, arms threaded with cotton-blue veins.

Joe drives up and down once, twice a day. Girls of every age and size and shape. Rotating. One group out in the morning, another group after five. Driving so close to them and looking for Pia, one of them comes over to him.

You want something, or you just looking?

A young girl, he says, with red hair.

Do we have any redheads?

The woman throws the question to the woman beside her who pretends to look over her shoulder.

No, she says. No redheads. But we do have a brunette.

Wiggling for him, laughing.

You don't understand – I'm looking for someone.

Aren't we all? the woman says.

Joe wants to save her.

Lovely girl like you,

although she tells him: I am not.

Wasting your life like this (unlacing his shoes), you're too good for it (socks and trousers).

Don't worry about it – Pia helping him to forget. There are worse things I could be doing.

But he cannot think of one (buttoning up his shirt afterwards), saying: how about I give you the key to my flat? So you can go there and have a bath when you want, cook yourself a meal.

I'm not always there, he says. I have another house. The flat is for when I am on business and it's too late and too far to go home. Lying idle so much of the time, he says, why don't you use it?

Pia hides the key in her coat pocket.

And sometimes, when she is supposed to be working, she unlocks Joe's flat and goes inside.

Some afternoons she watches movies – Katharine Hepburn and Spencer Tracy in black and white, sipping drinks and sparring. She drinks tea and eats ginger biscuits. Lies on the bed and listens to DJs delivering dedications:

This goes out to Kevin. With lots of love from Paula.

Pia wonders what it would have been like not to fall in love with her brother but with a stranger. Someone she did not know and who did not know her. So they could choose slowly, carefully, what they showed of themselves. So they could hide when they wanted to, pull back, say: that's enough.

Then move on to someone else, Pia thinks, try someone different. Try being with different people, being different people, having secrets she could tuck to herself and spaces inside her own head.

When Pia watches Luke breathing, sometimes, when he is sprawled on the floor or stretched out on the bed, and she sees his chest rising and falling, she feels as if it is her own chest rising and falling.

Sometimes she feels as if she and the drugs are in battle and Luke is their glittering prize.

The next time Pia sees Joe, he gives her a bracelet of rubies.

Not rubies, he corrects her, just coloured glass.

But they spangle. Blood-red, tulip-red, claret, burgundy.

She kicks off her shoes, starts to unbutton her cardigan.

No, he says. No. It's all right. I don't mean that.

Almost running from the room, like he is trying to get away from her.

I don't want a free gift, Pia says.

Joe asking her questions like: where do you come from? And: what is it that you want?

Sloughing away, trying to find—

Why?

Why what?

Why you?

Why not?

Joe asking as if all questions have answers, as if he believes such a thing.

Joe just wants to—

I just want to help – he tells his friend – even clumsily. Like

I'm her – swirling beer around the bottom of his glass, looking at it moodily – last chance. Like I can give her – hesitating – something.

Looking up at his friend now, taking a cigarette.

And your wife?

My wife? (As if Joe's wife entered into or was any part of this.)

What's the point in involving her? Joe asks his friend, and answers himself in the gap between them: no point at all.

questionnaire

For the first month of their relationship Joe bought Helen flowers. Carnations, she remembers – white and pink.

Then freesias, tiny yellow and purple handfuls and she loved them so much because of the smell and the paint-box-bright colours that after that he bought her only freesias.

They had been together six weeks when he gave her a bunch of dried flowers. Pale pink and dusky mauve, brittle as fish bones.

They'll last longer, he said.

And he was right except she did not want them to last, ugly, dried-out things gathering dust in the hall. She wanted fresh flowers as fresh reminders that he was thinking about her.

That was eighteen years ago – when Joe worked on the boats. He was away for weeks. Returning with stories and presents. She had never had such presents. He imagined other boys had loved her, but he was the only one.

For eleven months (the period between meeting Joe in the lift to her father's office and walking to him down the aisle) Helen had the feeling of being special. It was like suddenly realising she had an incredible talent for sing-ing/dancing/painting. Everything in her life had meaning because it had brought her to this point.

When he was away working as a fisherman, she tried not to think too much about what he might be doing.

One time asking him (because she had to): are there others – in other places? Girls who love you and think you are theirs?

Joe told Helen he kept her photograph by the bed in his cabin – before they were married and for many years after.

Joe. Joe and her. She had never felt so happy, so certain that things would turn out all right.

Helen's father owned Joe's ship. Owned lots of ships and Helen wanted Joe at home. A promotion. An office job.

They had been married for ten years when Joe got the flat in town.

He'd try not to stay away too often, he said, but convenience, he said, and travelling to the office made him so tired.

Helen read an article once about women whose husbands lived in different countries. They were separated from their husbands for large chunks of time, but their relationship was better for it – all the women in the article said so – except one woman whose husband left her. But he probably would have left her anyway. Anyway.

For years Joe stayed at the flat in town one night, at the most two nights a week. But recently Helen has noticed he's been staying out more and more.

Alone, Helen stretches out on the sofa and watches soap operas, has baths and leaves wet towels on the floor, goes to bed in a tracksuit and extra-rich (but hideous, blue) face cream.

But it all feels aimless. Helen is beginning to think she may as well not be married for all the time she spends on her own thinking about things.

Mainly Helen thinks how she has always wanted a child. Children are the special ingredient in a marriage. One of her friends calls them: the glue.

They stick you together, she says, for life.

Helen wants to be stuck to Joe. (Helen would like to be welded to Joe but glue will do.)

Joe does not want children. Never has. All the arguments over all the years. And always the same dead end.

I'm not good with children, he says.

How many times has she heard him say it: they drive me insane.

Helen wants to dazzle her husband. Wants to be one of those women whose husbands are in love with them for ever, never bored or frustrated, wanting to give them everything.

If Joe still loved her, Helen is sure he would not be so quick to call her:

foolish.

The first time he said it, she was shocked.

I'm not foolish. I just got it wrong.

Was he sorry that first time? Breaking into a smile like he was cracking a mirror.

Term of endearment, he said.

(As if.)

Brushing it aside.

Now he calls her foolish on a daily basis. That and more besides.

Running up and down the stairs several times a day, like it says in the magazines, to keep her tummy trim and a neat behind.

If he still loved her, it wouldn't be like this, Helen knows. This waiting for him to love her, feeling him always a breath away.

The other women talk about sex as something to be avoided, happy that their husbands are more interested in their car (or their golf clubs or their beer). But Helen wants to be the centre of her husband's universe. It is all she has ever wanted to be.

If there was another woman in his life she is sure she would know about it. There would be signs. Her woman's intuition would know. That is what they say in the magazines:

A woman's intuition is good and always to be trusted.

If only you can find it, thinks Helen, if you only know what you are looking for.

She just knows that she wants to be important to Joe.

(The magazines say: *you need to be important to yourself.*)

Helen borrows something in red lace from a friend—

Works wonders, her friend says.

Helen tries to imagine the wonders her friend is talking about, trying the underwear on in the bathroom every night for a week. Looking at herself in the mirror, trussed up like a turkey. She feels embarrassed.

She hides the shimmer of red lace under the sink. Not daring to walk into the bedroom in it. To stand under Joe's eyes like a too-sickly cake.

They go to a party and Helen wears a new dress and she feels pretty. Returning home, feeling hot in her body and calling to Joe shyly from the bathroom.

Standing by the sink in red lace.

He makes love to her slowly and it is good between them. Helen is sure (pretty sure) of that.

She feels like a person without a centre. That's how she describes it for the questionnaire in her magazine. Question one (out of eighteen): *how do you rate your self-confidence?*

Without my husband, Helen writes, I am a person without a centre.

It looks funny in black and white. Looks like the words (in her handwriting) are about somebody else. Not her. Not her and Joe.

Why do you want to change your life? (Question two.)

Because I have no life – no, I can't say that.

Because I want my husband to love me – no that can't be right.

Feeling hot behind the eyes, a tightness in her throat.

It makes Joe weary, she can see that. The fact that she tries so hard but still she is getting it wrong. The *it* is hard to define, but the words she eventually settles on are:

Being Joe's wife.

(In answer to question three about: *repeated mistakes you make*.)

Helen dyes her hair from yellow to dark brown.

Do I look different?

Joe looks hard at her noticing. Noticing nothing.

Not really. Smiling awkwardly. What is it this time?

Squashed. Like an insect between his fingers. She doesn't want to cry, doesn't want to start blubbering in front of him and have him say: I'm sorry, again – because sorry is besides the point. The point is that she is invisible to him. He makes her feel like she is disappearing.

(The incredible disappearing woman. *Puff of pink smoke.* She's gone. Applause and gasps from the audience. Off-stage whisper: it was all her husband's work.)

Freedom.

She writes that on the questionnaire under: *ways life has disappointed you?*

Lack of freedom and I thought I would feel more certain – Helen writes. Not always looking over my shoulder, copying somebody else who is getting it right.

Would Joe love another woman more?

Helen sees him at parties, comfortable always with other men's wives. Making them laugh, talking to them in doorways.

Joe says she imagines it. Says: I'm only being friendly.

Then why don't you speak to the husbands? Feeling churlish.

Women are more interesting, Joe says.

All women, or only some?

If he loved her more, she's sure she would not notice. What would she care if a housewife in a cocktail dress got her thrills from flirting with her husband? If Helen knew she had captured Joe's heart utterly, what difference could another woman make?

The way to a man's heart. Each month the magazines suggest something different. As if a man's heart is fickle, thinks Helen, or in need of constant surprise. As if a pastry or lipstick or well-rehearsed phrase can make a man love you.

But there are women out there – Helen knows – who are adored by their husbands. There must be something those women are doing right.

Helen convinces herself a yellow silk dress she sees in a shop window will be the way to Joe's heart. Buys it even though it makes her feel like a stranger.

All the rage, says the salesgirl, piling Helen's hair on top of her head. For someone special?

Helen glows. Yes. For someone special.

Taking the silk dress home, listening in the car to the soft crackle of its tissue paper. Feeling excited. Like a child believing in magic. Believing in all permutations of possibilities.

And dressed up in that dress and full make-up, sitting on the bed waiting for Joe to come home.

Eventually there is the telephone call.

Joe says: darling I'm sorry – I can't get back.

Looking at herself in the mirror, as she says: but Joe.

Thinking that she looks like a tulip that's fading away.

When Helen suggests to Joe that she stays in the flat in town with him some nights, she is sure his first look is one of anger. Irritation. It flashes across his face like a subliminal message to buy ice cream or a chocolate bar – just long enough to plant the idea in her head, but not long enough to be sure. Sure she saw it.

Why would you want to do that?

He is smiling at her now.

Aren't you happy here, in this house? Here you have all your things around you and your friends.

She doesn't want to say: I'm bored of my friends, sick to death of this house and the unlived-in way it feels. She doesn't want him to know that she will be listening to her friends' words sometimes, drinking a glass of wine and listening and she will see Joe's hands or his eyes. Joe is the only thing that matters. Joe and the feeling that he loves her. It is what keeps her spine erect, stops her head from crashing off her shoulders to the floor.

She says: It's just that when you are away, I miss you.

That is not giving too much away, she thinks, not sounding too—

(*Men* – the magazines say – *hate a woman who is desperate.*)

I miss you too, he says.

Really?

Yes, he says, of course.

One eye on her, the other still on his newspaper.

Throwing herself into his lap. (*Be spontaneous* – say the magazines. *Don't be afraid to do something different.*)

Kiss me Joe.

And he kisses her. Now surely if there was someone else, he would not be so quick to do that?

They think they have tamed him with a suit. These days Joe shaves every day. Goes to work in a car cleaned by the son of his neighbour. There are people who would call Joe a lucky man.

For lunch he has Swiss cheese on rye bread or pastrami with olives or fish in mayonnaise, a little carton of orange juice, a few green grapes in a serviette that his wife packs for him. Sometimes a little note. After all these years. She imagines it makes him feel loved. Imagines him smiling to himself, not—

ripping the note to shreds, dropping them like confetti into the waste paper bin.

All these years she has been loving him and all these years there's been someone else. Lots of someone elses.

Sometimes – often – Joe likes to pay for it. Buy it – buy her – a someone who doesn't want a complication. Sometimes she is pretty and that helps. But that's not the important thing.

Joe wants the feeling of being a conqueror. That slither spark of: I did it. That's what he does it for.

No time he likes a girl more than when she is pulling away. No moment he cares about her less than when, like Helen now, she hangs on to his coat.

Agreed to the suit and the desk and the swivel chair because, like Helen, he wanted an end to it. The girl in every – not quite but often, often – the girls love a man who says: I can't stay.

I want a proper marriage, she said.

What's that?

One where the husband goes with his wife to parties.

So it was all about parties and the face that one showed. But he had married her. Married her and made certain promises. And they meant something to him in those small, clear hours.

I must have married her for a reason. Perhaps – and his face wrinkles up with discomfort – to like myself better.

Sitting at his desk with charts and maps and graphs, speaking to a captain over a radio.

Fine seas

and imagining them as he speaks, the glint of sun like glass on the water. Those days when the ocean was a carpet of riches rolling him across them, when everything moved around his feet.

The neat little house, with so many things co-ordinating. A certain way the towels are to be placed, the sheet folded down, the cups piled on the drainer. Helen could make a spring field feel like a mown lawn just by the way she positioned things.

Style – she tells him – the magazines suggest she interject style. Which she dutifully does and her friends dutifully comment on and occasionally copy.

Some nights Joe walks the streets in the rain, not bothering to put up his umbrella. Some nights he sits in a bar until it closes, one drink, one lifting of the hand, one sip, gulp, swallow, swallowing into the next. And all the time, behind every gesture and thought—

a woman.

The moment before conquest, the moment just before when he knows – but not quite yet with a certainty – the thing is his.

A moment, a feeling on which to hang a lifetime?

A series of moments, perhaps.

Helen is lying in bed watching a husband and wife fighting on the television.

There has been a murder.

You never loved me, says the woman, looking at the gun she has just fired.

And, on the floor, her husband crouching over the body of the woman he loves.

Helen gets out of bed and walks across the room to her wardrobe. Selects a pink suit, shoes and blouse. Stepping out of her sweatshirt and woolly tights, painting colours on to her face.

It is eleven o'clock. Helen fastens her gold watch around her wrist, selects a gold chain for her neck, her favourite ruby and pearl ring. Shivering into her fur-collared coat.

There are reasons not to go:

It is late.

It is dark.

Joe may not be pleased to see her.

No. She will not think that. Will not think that, even though the thought presses against the front of her head.

He will be pleased, she thinks, to see me. I will slip into the bed beside him, slide my arms around his body and I will know then that he loves me.

Sitting in the garage, inside the car, turning on the engine, the heater, the stereo.

Adjusting the wing and rear-view mirrors.

Thinking: I could easily go back inside now.

Switching on the headlights.

Turning the headlights off.

She will go another night. She will be spontaneous, she will surprise him. Later in the week, she thinks, or perhaps the week after.

Some nights now, Helen sits in the car. Instead of propped up on pillows in the bedroom. She listens to news programmes on the radio. Tries to care more deeply about the rest of the world. But she is hurting.

And hurt is hurt, she thinks. Is starvation in the desert or being shot at by maniacs any more excruciating than this?

Feeling thick in the head now, everything hazy. Pouring another glass of wine, stretching out on the back seat of the car. Wishing Joe were here.

Some nights she sleeps in the car. Wrapped up in her coat and covered with blankets.

Some nights, when Joe calls, she does not answer the telephone. She tells him she was out. Out with friends.

smallness

The first time Joe goes to the flat and finds Pia sitting at his kitchen table, he feels embarrassed. She looks so at home.

Pia leads Joe into the spare room where a man is sprawling on the bed.

This is my brother Luke, she says. We got behind with the rent and our landlady threw us out.

And then: I'm sorry. We had nowhere else to go. It's only temporary.

Temporary?

Until we can find somewhere else so live. If we're in the way, she says. Please tell us. We can leave tonight, she says, if that's what you want.

But Joe cannot say that is what he wants. Not absolutely. Because many nights he is lonely here on his own. He goes through his paperwork, watches television, reads a book. But unless he has company, he goes to bed before he is tired.

A night or two won't matter, he says.

Joe thinks of Helen. An expression on her face, a gesture of her head, that look she has when she is trying to hide her feelings from him. The way she says: it doesn't matter.

When they both know that it does.

Recently Helen is around him like a feather duster. Brushing him up the wrong way, moving everything out of place.

Be yourself for God's sake, he often imagines himself shouting at her. Stop creeping around.

She would be devastated, he thinks, appalled.

The more he stays at the flat, the more Helen fusses. Sometimes when he is with her he feels that there is no air and he has to walk out of the room.

Where are you going?

To get a glass of water.

Finding Helen standing behind him.

She doesn't say: I'll come with you, and he doesn't say: get out of my way.

He says: I think I'll have an early night.

Good idea.

You go up then, he says. I'll have one more glass of wine.

Good idea, she says, I'll join you.

No, I've decided – I'm going to bed.

Following him, Helen says: there's no fun in drinking alone.

———————————

It is cold inside the car. In the wing mirror, Helen sees herself. There are lines around her mouth – and her eyes look sad, she thinks, like the sad eyes of a child.

She has just read the words: *my husband does not love me.*

An anonymous woman's words talking to her out of a

magazine but seeming as if they have come out of her own head and landed there in front of her: my husband does not love me.

When a man falls out of love with his wife, the usual response is for the woman to blame herself. But she has done nothing wrong, the magazine says.

The magazine provides a list of signs and Helen ticks them off in the box on the left.

A husband may begin to withdraw.

(Yes.)

He may be short-tempered.

Secretive.

The wife can get blamed for this.

The man may – but not always – be having an affair. The important thing to know is that you have done nothing wrong.

I have done nothing wrong.

Helen would like to believe the magazine, but she knows with every fibre of her being that if Joe does not love her it is her fault.

Helen has a pain in her stomach.

She turns the car engine on.

The lights.

The stereo.

Helen looks into the mirror without seeing her eyes.

The roads are dark and almost empty. A woman in a raincoat

walking her dogs. Three yapping bundles of fur, like toys that have come to life.

Joe will be pleased to see her.

Lighting another cigarette.

She will stay one night but no longer.

And if he asks her to stay? She will say no. Helen can hear herself telling him – which magazine do these words come from? – *I understand a man needs his space.*

Parking in the street. Windows mostly dark. The ones that are still light chequer the block in crazy paving.

Helen climbs the stone steps, feeling her bag on her shoulder and thin heels beneath her feet.

Telling herself: he will be happy to see me.

Pulling her body forward.

Pressing the button for the lift. Being carried up to the second floor.

Standing outside Joe's flat, Helen can hear noises. Voices. Music. She is sure she can hear a woman's voice.

Go home now.

Tapping on the door.

Louder voice in her head: *go home now.*

Calling Joe. (Quietly.)

Imagining the neighbours.

Feeling small.

Joe.

It is quiet now inside the flat and Helen feels the way she

did when her school friends played hide and seek and she was the one looking. Looking and looking.

Home. Safe. The lights, the sofa, the television. Helen touches them like landmarks, life buoys in a shifting sea. In her bedroom, everything is as she left it. Sheet folded down, bedside light on, a small pile of upended shoes on the rug by the wardrobe.

She double-locks the front door, but keeps the windows open. The sofa still bears Joe's imprint. She fits her body inside.

Joe tells her he was out.

Out? Helen says. I heard voices.

Voices?

I stood outside your door and I could hear people inside.

Joe says: you must have made a mistake.

No, Helen says.

Maybe you got out at the wrong floor and didn't realise because the flats all look the same.

No, Helen says, I checked.

But did she? Standing in the kitchen now with a cup of cold coffee in one hand and an ashtray in the other, looking at her husband and thinking: it was late at night, I was tired.

I was tired, she says, and yet—

Joe puts his briefcase on the kitchen table, takes out his newspaper, is about to walk away.

She says: it's true, I can't be sure.

When Joe falls asleep in front of the television, Helen wakes him gently.

You'll hurt your back, she tells him. Come to bed.

Prodding at his shoulder with her finger.

Whispering in his ear: come to bed.

Not yet.

Helen can't be sure if he is awake or talking in his sleep, so she says again: come to bed.

I'll be up later.

Do you want the light out?

Joe nods his head.

These nights are colder, sometimes, than nights when Helen is in the house on her own.

Waking at odd hours, remembering Joe is there, but not there with her. Putting a cardigan over her night dress, creeping down the stairs.

Joe.

Seeing his shape curved on the sofa, but he has put a jacket over his shoulders and his coat and her scarf.

Joe.

Trying to wake him.

Come up to bed now.

And hearing him groaning.
All right, he says. All right.

Lumpen there, beside her. So much like a stranger.

———————

Lying in Helen's bed in the darkness, Joe thinks of Pia. Not with lust but with longing. He thinks: I long for her.

He longs for Pia because he cannot predict what she will like. Because she is constantly in motion. Because he can watch moods flicker across her face.

It's her loyalty to her brother – hiding his drug-taking from Joe, his stealing, his temper.

Saying: I'll replace the vase. Saying: It was me – not Luke – that knocked it to the floor.

It's her size, her smallness in the vastness of his lounge – thin and white and seeming to fold in on herself. It is her hugeness in what feels like the smallness of his life.

It is because sometimes when she is crawling over his body, he feels as if she is a part of his skin.

away

Joe says: I want things to be better for you.

Hands dangling by his sides like gloves.

I care.

Saying the words for the first time.

I know it sounds strange. And you probably don't believe me.

Pia is standing there looking at him, head on one side like a bird.

I'm not like the others, he says. I like spending time with you.

I have to go now.

I know.

Luke is waiting for me.

Watching her assemble her bag and her coat.

See you later, she says.

Joe nods.

Feeling old now and tired. When she leaves the room the life – the sparkle – leaves with her. Nothing to do now but sit and wait for her home-coming. His home. Her coming. She makes his life feel like a home.

Pia likes the way Joe talks to her. Like she means something.

Heard a lot of the same words before. But not the way he says them. What if he means the things he says?

Luke is jealous.

Says: I don't like the way you look at him. Then, quietly: do you like him?

Pia thinks about the question before answering.

Yes.

There is a silence like a giant's yawning.

Much?

What?

The sound of his voice at last, though it's so quiet it startles her.

Do you like him much?

I don't know.

What do you mean by that?

I mean that I like him – standing up, feeling hot and restless now. I mean that he's kind and he treats me like—

Like?

She dare not tell him, sucking back the words, though they are fighting each other inside her mouth, jostling and colliding like marbles.

He makes me feel I matter.

The words jumble out anyway, clattering across the coffee table and on to the carpet.

And I don't?

Of course you do but—

It's too late, she knows it now. The damage done. He is like a wave drawing back across the sand, pulling away from her.

There is a difference. Between Joe and the others. It's not just the way he talks to her, the things he says. He feels—

Not just the flat, the ruby bracelet, the take-away Chinese meal dripping oil on to the carpet. All these things and something besides.

Less like a stranger, more like a friend. Less like selling part of her body and more like doing a favour for a friend. To make him happy. Liking it when Joe is happy.

Dinner with Joe in a restaurant one night. Napkins like towels. Everything stiff and bright. A yellow carnation on a long green stem bought from a woman who wishes them:

Happiness tonight.

Pia says: Luke and I have dreams. Where we'll end up. Somewhere hot. By the sea. In a hotel with a balcony and clean sheets every day.

And blue skies.

Blue, blue skies.

Other men. And gradually less of them. Joe keeps the fridge well stocked and leaves money in a tin – just enough. For Luke to buy the things he needs.

Luke out more and more. Buying and selling. Radios, car parts, pieces of jewellery exchanging hands in a seeming circle of I owe you to someone at the top.

Luke doesn't like her cutting down. Doesn't like them being dependent on one punter.

He's not a punter.

He is.

Voices rising.

What is he then?

I don't know.

Not a lover, Luke says.

No, not that, Pia says. But he won't throw us out on to the street.

How do you know that?

I just know it.

And what if he does?

He won't.

He would if he found out about us.

Joe can give himself a hundred reasons why he's doing it. And none of them make sense to him, not when he tries to find words. It is the common sense of his heart.

He wants to take Pia away.

Somewhere hot, he says. By the sea. Just for a few days.

Joe turns the coffee mug around and around in his hands. Sees a topless white china girl with the word Mona printed in red around her waist. One of Luke's mugs. His motor cycle magazines and cigarette butts all over the flat. And Pia's underwear is in lines across the bathroom, loops and curls of pink and greying white.

But when Pia says: yes, I'll come away with you—

Joe feels like a beneficiary. Against the odds, this strange girl sitting on his lap in his flat fills him up.

The travel agent shivers into her jumper.

Spain sir? she says.

Joe looks at Pia. Or Italy? he asks. Portugal? France?

He is looking at Pia as if she has a way of deciding, as if those places are more than words to her in an atlas.

Portugal sounds nice, she says. (Port makes her think of boats and ugal sounds like a sea bird, an Ugal.)

The woman books them two flights, a hotel with a swimming pool and a bedroom with a balcony looking over the mountains.

A contrast of modern coastal resorts, Pia reads from the brochure, and centuries' old fishing villages.

Vila de Sagres, says Joe, rounding Cabo de Sao Vincente, sailors and merchants lured by adventures and riches set on a course around Africa. Bound for new worlds.

The woman says: do you need currency?

And Joe pushes his credit card towards her.

Five hundred, he says. No, make it a thousand.

I don't want you to go.

Luke is hunched on the bed in the spare bedroom. He has a book on his knees, empty mugs, plates, bits of card and used matches spread all around.

I don't want you to go without me.

Joe sighs. No.

Seeing Pia standing in the kitchen doorway, shuffling her weight from leg to leg, head on one side.

No, Luke is not coming with us.

Because Joe feels uncomfortable, often, in front of Luke. Loses words when he tries to speak to him. Sounds like an idiot, inadequate.

No.

The way Luke walks around the flat in his boxer shorts. Helping himself to beer from Joe's fridge, crunching biscuits, flicking the television channels with the remote control – four three two four – until Joe wants to shout at him:

Haven't you got anything you want to do with your life?

Is it jealousy? Joe questions himself. Do I wish I could sit at home in my underwear eating biscuits? Or is it because he has Pia to look after him? Because she cares for Luke and not for me?

No, Joe says. No way.

His palms feel itchy, rough cotton of his trousers scratching at them. Wanting suddenly to cancel, to abandon the whole thing. A crazy idea. Him and this wiry girl on a beach somewhere.

And Helen. Sitting at home in front of the television night after night. He will take Helen on holiday, too. Some time soon. Make it all up to her.

Soon, thinks Joe, when he is over this girl and his life has gone back to normal.

Helen has set candles floating in a bowl. Joe can smell pot-pourri and a heady perfume oil.

Helen is drinking more than she used to. That must be her third glass of wine and she is slicing her food into tiny cubes and pushing them around her plate.

Are you all right? Joe asks her.

Yes, of course.

You're looking pale.

Am I?

I'm going away for a few days, Joe says. Out of the country. But when I come back, why don't we take a holiday together?

And Helen, running to sit on the arm of his chair, feels as if she is something solid and frozen thrust suddenly into the sun.

No work?

No.

No telephone calls?

No.

We'll get back to how it used to be.

I want that too, Joe says.

Pia is tender with Joe tonight, hesitant and slow. Lying on his back with his eyes closed, feeling the flicker of her tongue, a finger along his thigh.

And Joe is thinking of Helen. Helen with her scared dark eyes, saying:

Is this good? Am I getting it right?

All Joe ever wanted was for her to do what felt right to her, natural. But the words were an anathema to her.

Tell me Joe, what you like.

What he likes.

He can't tell her. It is as if the words, on leaving his mouth, would swell to the size of apples, melons, small countries. They would land on the carpet like bombs. Her hair would catch fire and her dress and the house.

It's fine – he always says to Helen. Because that is as honest as anything else he can say.

It is fine, honestly. I'm tired, shall I turn out the light?

Is this good?

The words in Pia's mouth light flames from his toes to the hairs on his head.

We're going to Portugal, she whispers the words against his neck.

She makes Portugal sound like a cave of treasure.

He will take Pia to Portugal and then he will return to his wife.

———————

Pia loads her bags into the taxi.

She has to run back inside the house three times, four, five.
The last being when they are a block or two from the house,
telling the taxi driver:

I must go back.

What is it this time? Joe asks.

My purse.

Your purse?

I left it on the bed.

Are you sure?

Yes, I know exactly where I left it. It won't take a moment to find.

All right – Joe says, not wanting to get the holiday off to a
bad start – be as quick as you can.

Luke is sprawling on the bed. Music loud.

Luke.

Pia stands in the doorway calling louder.

Luke.

He looks up but the music is still blaring.

Turn it down.

Mouthing: what for? Shrugging, looking away.

I need to talk to you.

Turning the music down herself.

I feel bad about leaving you.

So you've told me.

Will you be all right?

What do you think?

Telling Joe on the forecourt: I can't leave Luke.

He's not coming with us.

Then you'll have to go alone.

The taxi driver picks up his newspaper, meter clicking around.

Okay, says Joe. Shouting: tell Luke to be quick.

Watching Pia's new red sandals running away from him and back into the house.

In the taxi, Luke tells Pia about a film he watched the night before. Details, characters, scenes, wanting her to know all of it so when he says:

What do you think, should the man have murdered him or just taken his money?

Pia can say: the money should have been enough.

Luke is leaning back in the car, legs stretched out in front of him, hands on his knees. Taking up more than his third of the taxi, Joe thinks, looking away from Luke, looking out of the window. Not sure how this boy manages to crawl under and wriggle round inside of his skin.

At the airport, they discover there are no spare seats on the flight. But there is another flight leaving in the evening. For a few moments it looks as if Pia and Luke are going to take the first flight together, but Joe is adamant. He will have Pia to himself if only for a few hours.

Luke waves Pia off at the passport barrier.

See you in a few hours, Pia says.

Seven and a half hours, says Joe.

Walking through Passport Control into Duty Free – lines of liquor, watches, perfume, make-up, clothes.

Joe buys Pia a bottle of Rive Gauche. Wanting to hold her hand, her arm, to hold on to her somewhere. Feeling – frenzied. Like he's got a major decision to make, like a big wind is going to come and blow his life away.

Pia.

Yes?

Turning now to look at him. Clear brown eyes. Red hair in a ponytail.

Do you—

What?

Do you like—

What?

Do you like – going on holiday?

Joe shrinking up, feeling like an idiot as she says:

Yes.

An idiot. Wanted to say: me, Pia do you like me?

Taking her hand. Fingers fitting inside his. Walking across the lounge with giant strides.

Up in the clouds, bumping, slipping, shifting. Champagne bubbling inside of her. Pia looks out at the sky. Sky and more sky.

At Faro airport, Joe buys mineral water, a packet of chewing gum and a sun hat. Hails a taxi, agrees a fee, helps Pia slip inside while all around are marooned tourists.

Red and green streets. Yellow sun. Paint box scenes. Speeding around corners. Children and dogs roaming rubbled streets.

Nearly there.

The taxi driver's moustache glints gold in the sunlight.

Hotel Tropic.

He takes their bags inside where everything is shining: floors, desk, chairs, tables, uniforms and walls.

isosceles

Helen buys a new hat. Stiff straw, wide-brimmed.

Joe said he would take her to Rome.

We'll stand on the Spanish Steps and eat pasta in a back-street restaurant where we'll have to shout to be heard, he said. Buy yourself some new clothes while I'm away.

Helen has her hair cut and her nails manicured. Sitting very still in the high-backed chair while a purple-lipped teenager tells her that purple is more fashionable than pink.

But Helen likes pink.

Choosing a shade that reminds her of Bazooka Joes and sticky kisses with a boy in a back row.

The girl files her nails into points.

Would you like some extra glitter? she asks. One coat, on top?

Helen has got glittery pink nails and they make her feel jittery every time she looks at them – resting by her knee or on the bathroom tap. Helen feels foreign, exotic, unknown. Like when she was a child and she made up a secret life for herself – who she would say she was when she was famous and people wanted to know.

When Joe telephones her from Portugal, he sounds hurried and vague.

You arrived safely?

Yes.

Is the hotel nice?

Yes.

Can you see the sea?

What?

The sea. Can you see it from your room?

Yes.

That must be nice.

Yes.

Tell me something Joe.

What do you mean?

Tell me what it's like. Is the town pretty?

No.

Is the sun shining?

No, he lies again.

Joe imagines Helen sinking back into the sofa, staring at the walls.

Soon be us, he says. You and me on the Spanish Steps.

Was it Audrey Hepburn, Helen wonders, or Katharine, standing on those steps in a black and white frame?

I've always wanted to see the Spanish Steps, she says.

I know Helen, he says.

Joe turns back to the girl on the bed, flicking television channels with the remote control. A western, the news, an American talk show: four fat women and a man in a suit saying: how do you want people to view you?

As human beings.

One of the fat women is wearing metallic-brown lipstick.

A man in a checked shirt at the back of the auditorium stands up and waves his arms so they bring the microphone over to him.

Name's Richard, he says, smiling broadly into the camera. I just want to say – and he points to the stage and the women sitting on it – that you are all ugly as pigs.

Camera lingers on the woman's metallic-brown lips which are quivering. Big arms folded across her ample chest.

Was that your wife on the phone? Pia asks.

Yes.

Pia flicks the channels again, lingers on the scene of an operating table and a surgeon in white, pretty nurse by his side. And a pretty wife crying in the waiting room.

She's fine, says Joe. Don't worry about her.

I'm not, says Pia. Are you?

Luke opens his second box of duty-free cigarettes and takes another gulp of tequila. A mother has been wheeling her baby up and down the aisle next to him for almost an hour. The squeaking of the pram wheels is driving him crazy.

He would like her and the boys in shorts and the woman in a suit to stop moving. He would like his hands to stop moving and his chair and the room. Sometimes he blinks and it's all all right again: a long grey hall and the roar of aeroplanes, a round clock on the wall, minutes crawling by.

The rest of the time, the world is spinning too fast or he is running too slowly and there is no way for him to catch up.

The flight now boarding at gate 38 . . . Last call for Santa Lucia . . . a little boy in a duffel coat has lost his mum.

The woman opposite Luke is reading a magazine. On the cover large letters announce: my husband ran off with my sister. And – in spidery type underneath – but he came back to me. The woman is engrossed, her fingers making little circles around her mouth as she reads.

———

Pia does not want to walk along the beach or sit by the pool or have sex with Joe in the shower. Pia wants room service. Tinned peaches and toast, a silver pot of tea and hand-painted cups. She wants to spread everything across the bed.

Let's pretend, she says, that we are having a grand party.

But Joe does not know how to play now-we-are-rich and he just looks at her. Alone with her for – he looks at his watch – four hours now. Alone in a blue room in Portugal and she wants to play games.

If Luke were here he would wrap the bed cover around him, he would swagger out on to the veranda, he would know how to make it fun. Joe has not even taken his shoes off. Pia wishes Luke were here or she was on her own and Joe was far away.

Saying: kiss me Pia.

And she wriggles away from him, goes into the bathroom.

Pia does not want to be touched by him. Not right now. Splashes her face with cold water. Looks in the mirror and sees Gerard.

This has not happened for a long time. She rubs her face roughly with the towel but he is still there: puffy eyes, potato nose, thin lips. He is watching her as she goes back into the bedroom and says:

Joe, will you just hold me?

He is watching as Joe wraps Pia inside his arms.

Counting the hours until Luke comes. Thinking about Gerard and Sam and the fisherman, thinking about all the ways things go wrong. Luke pulling pulling somewhere deep inside of her. From the other side of a room, a street, a continent. Counting the hours but hours do not mean anything. Time cannot be measured externally. It changes with the way she feels.

Lying on the bed, listening to the gloop of the swimming pool's filter and crows in the trees. Sometimes Pia feels big, so big Joe will never be able to touch all of her. Other times it is as if she is made of sticks and paper. Nothing to keep the wolf out or anything good in.

Joe likes to hold Pia. It's the one time she does not say: stop looking at me. He likes to look at her, the pale pockets around her eyes.

Sometimes the words: I love you sit in his mouth. If he said them he would feel an idiot. And anyway that is not the truth. It's not love, of that he is convinced.

But what else is there to call it? He wishes the five hours they have alone here together were five hundred or even five thousand. He wishes his heart would stop hammering, wishes his hands were inside of her clothes.

Stop it – she is pushing him away – I don't want to.

The light is too bright, she says, and I don't like the pillow.

The pillow?

I can see a stain.

A stain?

Yes, there – pointing at it but not touching it. Curling her knees up, her arms and body away from him and into the wall.

Take it away.

He puts the pillow on the floor, under the bed.

Gone.

He is laughing. Arms flung out like he is a magician and he can make things disappear – get rid of Gerard standing in the doorway; one blink and he is gone, another and he is vivid as day.

He is moving towards her. Joe shifting across the bed and the sheets rouche up under him. His hand on her arm feels like something burning. She would endure it if she could.

Please don't touch me.

They only have a few hours before her brother arrives. And then he will lose her to Luke. He always does. And he shouldn't care. Of course a sister is going to love her brother. But there is something else. He can't find the word for it – an edginess that sits between them, it is like still air before the beating of wings, like the millisecond before an explosion.

What's the matter? he asks her.

Nothing.

But she is pulling away from him as surely as if she was running from the room.

Is it something I've done?

No, Pia says.

She walks away from him and into the bathroom. He hears the click of the locking door.

He has been waiting an hour for her. An hour and fifteen minutes. Sitting on the bed in his bathrobe, wandering out on to the veranda to commiserate with the trees.

Won't you come out now?

Ear to the bathroom door, trying not to sound pleading.

Pia will you talk to me?

Say something.

Anything at all.

Leave me alone. The words come out small and flat.

Pia – Joe is as close as he can get to the door – this is agony.

In the bathroom, Pia makes little razor cuts in her arm. She is cutting a pattern. A box surrounded by more boxes, divided up into triangles. Isosceles triangles. The word isosceles over and over in her head.

There is red and there is sharp pain and there is the word isosceles, all of it strange and more remote to her the longer she sits there. Bottom on marble, knees towards chest, arm leaking slowly.

There is a man in the room next door and she can hear him moving around. Every now and then he comes to the door and speaks to her. When he is there, she is very quiet. Holding her breath, hand pressed to arm so that he cannot hear her bleed.

Pia come out.

The words replace isosceles and run like a mantra in her head.

PiacomeoutPiacomeout.

Please.

Pleasepleaseplease. It is a thin word, she thinks, long and thin, chugging across the blank screen of her mind like a train.

When he goes away, she has to wash her arm to remove the smudges, to see the pattern again. It is a good pattern.

She likes it. Wonders whether to try to copy it on to her other arm.

There is yellow behind the window. It seems to be trying to get into the room.

It is hard to stand up, she has to hold on to the wall to stop herself from falling down. Pia stands still for a moment, waiting for the giddiness to pass.

Toilet, sink, bidet, bath. Negotiating a path between them to the window. Climbing on to the bidet to press her arm against the frosted glass, to cool it down, change this pain for another kind.

She is so quiet in there. He wishes he could see her. Before, he wanted to touch her, now he wants only to see her. He does not know her. Not what she thinks or wants, not who she is or how she feels. But he cannot bear to be separated from her.

Should he go to the door and try to talk to her again? Ridiculous. He should go outside into the sunshine and have a swim.

Joe stands on the veranda looking down on the pool. Pink and brown shapes on floral sun-loungers, squiggles of coloured fabric hiding as little as possible, maintaining privacy. *Privacy*. And here he is shut away from the girl that he—

For a moment there is the word, prostitute. She is a prostitute. She has no right to be doing this to him. And with it comes an anger, a swift sweeping anger that takes him back to the door again, fist clenched tight.

Come out of there.

He shoves his fist into his pocket. How dare she do this to him, how dare she make him feel this way?

He should go for a walk along the beach or drink a Scotch at the bar or sit alongside one of those brown, barely private bodies and forget all about her.

Come out now.

He has a right to demand this. A perfect right. Joe has the beginnings of a hangover. It hurts to keep his eyes open. All the things he has done for her. All his kindnesses. And down there, a hundred happy holidaying couples. She is wasting their precious time. She is making it all go wrong.

water wings

The sun is setting. Joe is still in his bathrobe on the veranda. He has finished the bottle of Scotch but it has barely touched the sides of his misery and wanting.

Down by the pool, they are laying out tables and chairs for the night's entertainment. A child in water wings is bobbing still on the surface of the pool like an enormous insect.

A knock on the door.

It's me. It's Luke.

Opening the door.

How happy Luke looks, how young and happy and loved, loved, loved. I am drunk, thinks Joe, after all.

Where's Pia?

Luke is barely inside the room and he is looking for her, eyes scanning the bed, the sofa, the veranda, the locked bathroom door.

In the bathroom.

Joe puts his hand on the wall to steady himself.

Luke puts down his rucksack, takes off his denim jacket.

Got a drink?

Over there.

Joe tilts his head towards the mini bar and has the feeling it will come off his shoulders and spin across the room. Spin across the room and land, splat, on the bathroom door. Then there will be just the two of them. Maudlin old man, he wants to laugh, cry, shout at the top of his voice. She has been in there so long and all the time he has been stretched taut as an elastic band.

Luke positions a bottle of beer underneath the dressing table and hammers off the lid.

Cheers.

He is smiling. In good spirits. Joe lowers himself on to the sofa, looks at the coffee table.

She won't come out.

With one movement, it seems, Luke is across the room and by the bathroom door.

Pia, it's me.

Using a voice Joe has not heard him use before.

Pia, it's Luke. Are you all right?

Pia is in an enormous aquarium where gentle fish are feeding on seaweed. Everything is in slow motion, slow liquid motion. Tentacles slip and slide around her arms and legs, calling her into the belly of an octopus where she will at last be safe.

Pia, it's Luke.

She hears his voice but she cannot move towards him, liking it where she is, wishing she could tell him she is all right.

Pia, can you hear me?

Sliding into the purple heartness and she would be gone if not for the sound of Luke's voice. The thought: she could go back for him, pull him in here with her so that they can both rest.

Trying to say his name.

Luke.

But her mouth fills with water.

All she can do is swim and breathe.

Luke is kicking at the door. Throwing his full weight against it.

Joe tries to stand but his legs buckle beneath him. He would like another drink but the bar is too far away.

She is slumped in the bidet.

Blood on the porcelain and marble and her hitched-up sundress.

Blood on her arms and her thighs and matting her hair.

Luke picks Pia up and carries her into the bedroom. His head against her head.

Saying: it's all right.

Whispering to her gently.

I'm here.

Lying her on the bed.

Stroking the hair from her face. Ripping a towel and binding her arm with the ragged strips.

Call a doctor.

Turning to Joe with a face totally altered. Eyes blazing.

Do it now.

Holding the telephone in his hand like something awkward and unfamiliar, Joe speaks into the mouthpiece.

Room one hundred and eight. We need medical help.

Feeling like a character in a movie. Automatic, scripted.

Turning to Luke, saying: I didn't realise. And: how could I?

But Luke is aware now only of his sister. Shutting Joe out as totally as Pia did all those hours before.

The doctor applies sticky strips to the back of Pia's left arm.

Lost a lot of blood, he says. But it's not too bad.

He injects liquid into Pia's vein. Leaves a plastic pot of painkillers on the bedside table.

Which of you is her nearest of kin?

Luke says: I am.

Are you insured?

Joe finds his voice. I will pay for it.

The doctor looks at him.

Are you the girl's father?

No, says Joe.

She is asleep now. Looks peaceful.

Joe feels like an outsider. Outside of her life.

Sitting on the slatted chair on his expensive veranda. Not so different to his chair in his living room, whenever Luke is around.

Joe thinks: I should have gone in for her myself. I should

have realised. Quiet for so long and all I did was pace the room and drink.

She sleeps for a long time. Luke laid out on the bed beside her.

Joe orders another bottle of whiskey from room service and from time to time he stands up and crosses the long expanse of marble between them. The clink of whiskey bottle against glass disturbs their silence like a bell.

Are you hungry?

Luke shakes his head.

Feeling useless, Joe dials room service again. Orders two club sandwiches – the most familiar-looking items on the laminated menu.

And coffee, Joe says – he is feeling nauseous now – and make it strong.

Stars speckling the warm night.

When Pia stirs, they both turn towards her. She shifts in her sleep. Throws her bandaged arm out above her head.

Joe can hear the grinding of Luke's teeth.

They drink their coffee in silence. The sandwiches lie uneaten on a hand-painted plate.

When Pia wakes, she curls in towards Luke's body and he rocks her gently, speaking so quietly Joe cannot hear.

It was Gerard again.

Sshh, it's all right, I'm here now.

Will he ever go away?

He's gone now, isn't he?

Yes.

You're safe. You can go back to sleep.

This time when Pia sleeps, Luke slides his arm out from under her and goes into the bathroom. Joe can hear the hiss of the shower.

Alone in the bedroom with Pia, Joe wants to sit beside her. But he feels he has no place there. No place with her at all.

Luke cleans the bathroom so that the marble gleams. Red rivers sucked down plug holes, washed completely away.

Luke stands under the shower and it is like standing under hot needles. Chafing his thin white body with a towel, wanting to pummel the white-tiled walls.

In her dream, Pia has died and gone to a place just like the one she left behind. Except. There are no floors and no ceilings and everything keeps shifting around.

Luke.

She is calling to him.

Luke, Luke.

But she has no voice.

A nurse with vacant eyes says: never mind now, hush hush.

And she pats Pia's arm with a hand like a cobweb.

There, there.

And there's a needle in her hand and Pia is shaking her off and opening her mouth so wide her face splits apart.

And still they wrap her up in sheets and tell her: it's all going to be all right.

Waking on the bed and thrashing. Hearing her own voice.

Luke, Luke.

Her own voice screaming.

And the man leaning over her could be a character in her dream world because there is only one face that can make her feel real.

Joe is back out on the veranda, smoking a cigarette. Candles lit now on the tables around the pool. A suited band playing tinkle music. A man's crooning voice: summer breeze makes me feel fine.

There is a chill in the air. Click of cicadas.

Joe wants his jacket. Sees it on the chair in the bedroom. Sees Pia's and Luke's heads together now, on the pillow. They are whispering. Never has Joe felt so alone.

———————

Joe goes to sit on the bed beside Pia but sits instead on the chair.

I'm sorry, Pia says.

Joe shuffles the chair closer towards her; feels like an insect, crossing the floor on six mismatched legs.

Does it hurt a lot?

Not too much.

Looking at the bedspread's swirling gold pattern then at his sandals, asking: was it something I said?

Oh no, she says, not you. Please don't think it's about you.

Joe finds a spare blanket in the cupboard, a candy-striped pillowcase, a pillow that smells of someone else's cologne. Hunched up on the too-short couch, listening to Pia and Luke whispering. And downstairs the last few people around the pool, sipping night caps, dangling feet in the turquoise water.

the water's language

The mountains are many colours: green, pink, brown, black. In their shadows there are faces. The air thick with birds. A stillness. The sounds of dogs. The quiet murmur of the men on the building site. The tops of the trees sunlit.

The morning after. Tender, punctured. Feeling her whole body is a bruise and her skin too thin.

They sit around the breakfast table: Pia, Luke and Joe feeling like an old man on holiday with—

To the other guests they probably look like his children.

Wanting Helen suddenly. Violently. Wanting Helen. Wanting to fit back into all that.

Squinting at them through sunglasses, Joe sees leg resting against leg, their hands touching as they speak. Pia is eating an ice cream and it drips on to her stomach. She is wearing a bikini, a tiny white and black bikini with flowers that look like strawberries over it. And it is so hard for him to stay in his deckchair while Luke is between them, blocking her out as surely as an umbrella in the sun.

Hot, he says for the fifteenth time.

Yes, Pia agrees.

Pia feels the sunlight in her legs, inside her legs, yellowing her blood and filling up all the spaces inside her.

Looking out at the pool and the people sunbathing around her. Leather bags and mules and hardback books, sunglasses sparkling with chips of diamond – or is it glass? Biting on watermelon and mango and fat black figs.

Luke comes back from the kiosk carrying more ice creams, more cans of beer, more sun cream.

Smell this, he says, thrusting a plastic bottle under Pia's nose.

Liquorice, she says.

Yes, he says, imagine lying back in the sun and stinking of liquorice. Everything is six times cheaper at the kiosk, he adds loudly. All these idiots paying over the top every time they wet their lips.

Joe sees an old woman, the rolls of fat around her belly like red-painted tyres, thick lines of sun cream along her thighs now that it is too late to prevent them from burning.

Pia is noticing how white Luke is, so white that his skin looks blue. How blue he looks, hunching in on himself, pale blue veins on his back.

He looks unhealthy.

Saying: you look unhealthy.

Everybody else looks – she whispers it – well-fed.

Plumped-up, Luke corrects her.

I want to get away, Luke mumbles. Soon as we can.

Smiling at and through me, thinks Joe. Like she did the first time. Like they always do.

Luke has a name, a street name and a telephone number scribbled on a piece of paper under the word gold.

Don't go.

The same words – England, Portugal, inside Pia's head or out loud.

Luke says: you don't understand.

I do – don't go.

Got to—

When will it ever stop?

Biting back the words too late and he's gone, slipping through the door like a shadow.

And Joe – out on the veranda in the fading light. Sitting beside him on the slatted chair, watching stars puncture the sky.

He pours her a glass of wine. Sweet and cold in the gathering darkness. He reaches for her hand and she lets him hold it.

A shooting star tearing across the sky like a rocket.

Did you see it?

Yes.

And just for a moment – this moment – this is the hotel by the sea of her dreams. For a moment she is in exactly the right place, feeling only good things. And it is not Joe who breaks the rule that Pia set for herself when working. It is Pia.

Looking at his face – familiar, known now, he does not frighten. Kissing him.

Because she feels like it. Because she wants to give him something.

Joe says: I wish there was another way we could have met, done it differently.

Wanting and not wanting to hear him talk. Sometimes Joe's words make her feel empty. How empty it all is and her here, wasting her chance at a life.

I wish I could make your life different. Somehow. Make a difference.

Stop talking Joe.

The future, he says. Where do you imagine yourself?

I don't know.

Ten years from now?

I don't know.

Five then?

Shrugging.

What about three?

Three years into the future. Imagining herself there. Seeing the sea and the mountains. Seeing – looking for – Luke. She is looking around for Luke. Looking but she cannot see him. He is not there.

Saying: I don't know.

Because she doesn't want Joe to know, does not want to name it, to speak it, the possibility.

Luke finds the dealer, the street, the man. Taking a taxi back to the hotel. All the time thinking of the swift heat before it enters his body, like he is wearing its echo.

The slow heat of the day. A group of women in the shell of a building, curved red piles of bricks. A pink rose bush.

Pia gives the woman who cleans the room an orange. The woman says no, takes Pia into the lounge and shows her she wants bread. Will not cut it for herself, although Pia lays it all out for her – bread knife, bread, butter knife, butter. Pia cuts her a hunk and the woman eats it dry, sitting on the edge of the sofa next to Pia's plastic bowl of laundry.

On the street, a skinny red dog slumped over the body of her dead child. She is shivering but also shielding, curved over, teeth chattering. Pia buys milk and the dog licks the drops as they fall from the plastic carton. Pia buys more milk, three eggs, a loaf of soft white bread, feeds the dog by hand crouching down with her in the street, her small beige pup between them.

What to do? a stallholder says. The life.

Shrugging but looking sad, amused and sad, much sadder than amused.

She does not know her child is dead, that's why she keeps licking it, to warm it. I will take it away, he says, in a while.

Two eagles flying above their heads in concentric circles,

looping round and round, interconnected. Sky empty now, pale washed blue.

Pia dreams she is sitting in a wicker chair watching the sun set in shades of orange. And in between the stillness of the trees the knowledge she is alone. She wakes with a panic, reaches for Luke. Safe and warm still, beside her.

I love you.

I know you do – half asleep – I don't need you to tell me.

But I needed to tell you, breathing the words into his warm back. Needed to hear the words out loud.

And a madman on a street corner, talking to the sky.

Preacher, he says, nauseating, born-again preacher, shove it down your throat, I've found it, what you're looking for, blissed out on fucking nothing man – nothing. That's what it means and everything going round and round again in circles, wheel of life and death and born a – here we are again and what is right with the world and wrong with my head?

He says: I want to spread a message, let them know at some point it gets good, better than good, better than they imagine. Go down – want them to know it's part of it – coming right back up if only they'd believe. Believe in themselves.

Oranges dangle in the trees like earrings, delicious cold segments on her tongue late at night when the dogs take over barking, echoing, seeming to press in on the walls and the baby in the next room screaming.

Falling asleep in the sun, Pia dreams herself on the mountain again. Trees that ripple in the daytime and whisper in the night. Bright green parrots flaring for a moment over the trees, wings fanning. Butterflies that dance colours in front of her eyes.

She calls out for Luke but he is not with her. Not in the mud house behind her, not up in the pink mountain. Alone on the mountainside with a chair and a garden. And in her dreams she does not miss him because she knows he is safe.

Watching the weather change like moods. The shattered sky. How yellow the light in the sugar canes.

On the beach, waves leap around Pia's legs, knocking her over, running round and round.

Calling to Luke: come in the sea, it feels fantastic.

Too cold – Luke who put one big toe at the water's edge and ran back from the tongue of white foam curling across the sand behind him.

Too cold and too wet.

What about you?

Calling now to Joe. Joe feeling paunchy under Luke's eyes. Not wanting to be seen running across the sand towards her.

Just tell us, says Luke, when you've had enough and want us to leave.

And Luke's words sound like a dare to Joe. Like Luke is intending to push him to his edge.

Pia and Joe lie on their backs in the sea. Arms and legs stretched out like the points of a star. The water muffles their ears so that all they hear is the water's language. Low gloops and whirrs and a continual hummmm.

Eyes squeezed tight against the sun so when they open them they flash and they feel blinded. The water shifts over their bodies like a loose dress.

Luke hangs back and there is a pile of shells by his feet, domed by a child who did not care whether the shells were perfect or just fragments of bigger things. A patchwork of corners and ends of shell and as it catches the light, he can see the face the child has drawn inside it. Stooping to scatter the shells with his hand, to hear their sound.

Swimming away from Luke, feeling the water under their outstretched arms, kicking with their legs. Long, slow strokes. Part of each wave and the sea and the whole ocean coming together, the ripple of their wrists sending tremors for miles, interacting perhaps with an octopus or sea lion, a deep-sea whale or minute mollusc. For a moment feeling connected to all things.

And to nothing, thinks Pia. And to no one.

rooms

It was Joe's voice. The new sound in it. Helen does not want to wait. Rome seems too far away. What if this moment passes, if it disappears and she doesn't act on it, she may be sorry for the rest of her life.

Ordering the ticket over the telephone—

To Faro, on the first flight you have.

Helen boards the plane in her pale blue suit, clutching her matching valise, her sunglasses and hat.

So excited at the thought of seeing Joe. Also so afraid.

She would not have found the nerve – if not for the way he sounded on the telephone. Gentler than she has heard him in months, like he means the things he says about taking her to the Spanish Steps and beginning to love her again.

Clutching her tiny champagne bottle to herself in the air, sipping the bubbles.

First time in Portugal? the man beside her asks.

Yes, says Helen.

There are the beginnings of stubble on his chin; he fidgets with his glass.

Where are you staying?

Hotel Rameses. I'm not sure which hotel my husband is in,

Helen explains, because he did not tell me – biting the rim of her glass. I imagine the hotels are close together, she says brightly. I'm sure I will find him.

Bundled inside a taxi with the man from the aeroplane because he says he can drop her at her hotel on his way.

Wives think these trips are all fun and girls, the man laughs, as if we have the time to do anything – he opens his arms in a wide gesture – anything except work and eat and sleep.

Standing in the reception of the Hotel Rameses.

Room for one?

It is the way the receptionist says it, makes Helen feel she has to defend herself.

I am meeting my husband here, she says. I am not here on my own.

Helen is sitting on the hotel bed and the room feels so large and empty after the porter has gone and the door closes with a click. Scouring the names of the hotels in the phone book.

Telephoning the Hotel Marissa.

Asking for: Joe Reed.

What nationality?

British.

Helen hears the receptionist sighing through the receiver.

No, I'm sorry, she says. No one of that name here.

Cartoon on the television: mouse with a sombrero and glasses, running up and down and waving at her.

Helen decides to take a walk, not bothering to change her clothes or wash her face because she wants to get out of the room as quickly as possible. She will find Joe soon, she tells herself, so no reason to unpack her suitcase or try to make the room look homely.

Grabbing her bag and jacket from the chair.

Walking out in the sunshine and stopping, for a moment, to feel it on her face. Turning her head back now and up, up to get as much of it as she can. Warm on her hands too and in the gap between her trousers and her sandals.

At a café across the street, Helen orders a cappuccino, sitting outside where she can watch the people go by and imagine she is one of them – that woman perhaps, with sun-bleached hair scraped back off her face, and her body so trim in a bikini top and shorts. Her companion seems to be doting on her, pointing out landmarks and guiding her with his arm.

Stirring sugar into her cup, Helen allows herself to imagine, for a moment, the way that would feel.

And where is Joe?

There are so many strangers, so many people she can feel herself panicking. What if she doesn't find him? What will she do here alone?

Helen walks in and out of hotel receptions, through revolving doors, saying thank you to receptionists and porters.

No Joe Reed staying here, are you sure?

Sipping lemon tea in a foyer. Buying a book at a kiosk shop because it helps when she has to sit alone.

Flicking through the paperback, eyes picking up individual words – honeymoon, love-sick, equation.

Wishing for Joe.

He is not sure it is her. In fact he is positive it is not. It cannot be her, she is back in England in their house. He spoke to her only last night. Last night. It can not possibly be her.

Joe is hiding behind a palm tree – a palm tree, he thinks, for Christ's sake. Feeling like a caricature – the unfaithful husband; sketched on to a thousand joke post cards: guilty man hiding himself away.

Coming out around the side of the plant, Joe thinks he recognises Helen's handbag. Looking at the woman from the back and her hair is the same colour as Helen's. Coughing so that she will turn around, but she moves only slightly so he cannot see her profile, only the shape of her chin.

The receptionist is calling the woman across the foyer, waving to her, beckoning her over to the desk.

And the woman walks like Helen, slightly loping, as if her shoes hurt.

I have found what you're looking for.

The receptionist is smiling at the woman, smiling like she has found buried treasure.

Your husband's room number, she announces, is room one hundred and eight.

Joe watches Helen moving over to the elevator. Joe knows the thing to do is approach her. Call out to her, stop her walking inside. But he cannot move. He watches the doors close.

Telephone up to the room, I must warn them, Joe tells himself. Looking for a telephone and seeing only the one on the receptionist's desk.

Running through the reception and into the street. Hailing a man with a horse-drawn carriage.

Take me around the block.

Around the block?

The man is wearing a battered straw hat.

Yes, a few streets or so, says Joe.

What do you want to see?

Joe jumps into the carriage.

Just go, he says impatiently.

———————

Mrs Reed?

Pia feeds the woman's name back to her through the closed door.

Did you say your name was Mrs Reed?

Yes, says Helen. That's what I said. Is my husband there?

Who is your husband?

Joe Reed.

Helen is tapping on the door again.

Is my husband in there?

No, says Pia. He is not.

Helen does not mean to cry, turning away from the locked door, biting down more words.

The receptionist seemed so certain. Room one hundred and eight, on the second floor.

Helen's legs won't carry her back to the lift. Five hours she has been looking. She has not eaten anything since the plane and she drank a lot of champagne and it's so hot – suddenly the tears are falling and Helen is sobbing and she cannot stop.

Pia hears her on the other side of the door and eventually she opens it. Sees the older woman crumpled in the hall, her head on her knees.

Do you want to come in?

Is my husband there?

Helen looks up and sees a girl. She is a child. Spindly in a T-shirt and shorts. Freckles along her arms.

No, says Pia. But he will be back soon.

Back soon?

Yes, says Pia. Do you want to come in?

Wanting to ask the girl: who are you, to Joe?

Wanting to hear it from Joe.

Helen is sitting in the untidy lounge. Sunlight dancing on the pool and the girl hovering around her. There is a bandage around her arm.

Can I get you a drink?

Yes, Helen says, thank you.

Lemonade with ice?

Just a child, Helen thinks again.

When will Joe be back?

I'm not sure, Pia says. He went for a walk.

Helen hears a noise in the bedroom.

I thought you said my husband is not here.

Helen is standing up.

He's not.

Well who is it in the bedroom?

Luke staggers out in a T-shirt and one sock.

Who is this?

This is Luke, my brother.

Luke looks up at the woman and smiles. Hair falling over his eyes.

Do you want breakfast?

Breakfast? It's five o'clock in the afternoon.

Good afternoon, Luke says.

Helen would leave. Except. This is Joe's room and so, by rights, it is her room. She belongs in here. Not them.

She would leave. Except. Her room at the Hotel Rameses is no more her room than this one. Nowhere to go. A long way from home.

———

Pia and Luke walk in the sea. Silver ribbons of water curling over their toes. Lying back on the sand, letting the sky swim over them. Watching the shape-shifting and the shadows, Pia feels a crab burrowing at her feet. Luke shines his torch, lighting up the crab's shell. Turquoise speckles in all that greyness

Time to leave.

He throws a stone into the water and the sound ripples in the darkness.

We need money, he says. What about Joe?

What about him?

How much has he got?

What are you talking about?

Taking Joe's money – Luke is drawling at her. What do you think I'm talking about?

No, says Pia.

No? Luke is incredulous.

No, says Pia. He is like a friend.

Like a friend?

I don't want to steal from him.

He won't miss it, Luke says.

silence

Helen seems different, thinks Joe. Standing in the centre of the room, her hair falling out of its clips and her eyes flashing.

Who are they?

They're friends of mine.

You lied to me.

I didn't lie to you.

You are lying to me now. Who are they?

People I met.

Why are they here? Why are you here?

I don't know, says Joe, why the girl is so important to me. But she is.

Running his hand through his hair.

Since I met her.

Pacing, pacing.

Can't think of anything but her. Do you know what that's like?

Helen's face is damp, droplets of sweat sitting on her face powder.

What is it like?

Helen is baiting him to tell her.

It's like—

Joe hesitates. Helen is not the right person for him to tell but he has held it in for so long, the way that he feels about Pia, and he wants to speak the words aloud, wants somebody to hear them, to make them change shape.

It's like I know her.

You know her?

Like I've always known her.

Don't tell me, says Helen – recalling a magazine list of excuses erring husbands most frequently use – she feels like a part of you.

You tried to stop it, Helen continues, but it was bigger than you.

Remembering another sentence from the list: you still love me but – let me guess – you want her, too.

It's not like that.

Oh really?

It's not just sex.

Sex – now he has said it – he has had sex with that girl—

She's just a child.

Not a child, she's seventeen.

Seventeen.

Helen starts to cry. Shoulders heaving. Lines of mascara dividing up her face.

Joe says: I'm sorry.

What about Rome? Helen says. What about the Spanish Steps?

We can still do it, says Joe coming to stand beside her.

Not like I imagined, wails Helen. Never like that.

———————————

Helen has cleaned the mascara off her face and rearranged her hair by the time Pia and Luke return so that when she opens the door to them and says:

Come in,

they cannot be sure what Joe has told her.

Walking into the room, Pia feels it is Mrs Reed's hotel room now. Feeling like they are a couple she is visiting and she needs to be well-behaved.

We're leaving, Pia says.

That would be best, Helen says.

We'll pack, Luke says. It won't take long.

In the bedroom, stuffing their clothes back into their bags, picking up books and magazines, after suns and sun lotions.

Quick, says Luke. Where does he keep his wallet?

In his jacket pocket.

Where's his jacket?

Pia's eyes scan the chair, the bed.

In the other room.

Luke starts rummaging through the bedside table – sees Joe's watch and wedding ring. Puts them in his pocket and continues to look.

You can't take those.

Be quiet – Luke's voice is a whisper. We might need them.

Moving aside Joe's passport and finding an envelope stuffed with notes.

Got it.

Luke puts the wad inside his jacket pocket.

Leave some, says Pia. Don't take all of it.

Yes, all of it.

Luke is determined.

Gathering up their bags they walk back into the other room.

Don't go, says Joe.

Helen says: Joe, what are you saying?

Don't go, Joe says it again. I want you to stay.

Pia looks at her shoes.

Thank you for everything, she says.

She is still not looking at him.

Where will you go?

We'll find a hotel.

Do you have any money?

Money?

Helen is indignant. Watching Joe reach for his wallet.

Here take this.

Thrusting a pile of notes at Pia.

I don't want it, Pia says.

Of course you want it. You need it.

Joe tucks the notes in the pocket of Pia's jacket.

And as she stands by the door, Joe says it again:

please stay.

And Pia says again: we can't.

Luke is pulling at her arm, standing in the hallway.

I have called the lift, he says.

Running through the reception hall, bags banging against their legs, Pia and Luke running out into the early evening and all the streets are lit up and in the distance the sea appears to be shining.

Running along the edge of the sea, through the foam high-lighted by the moon.

Free, says Luke.

And his happiness ignites her like the fuse to a Catherine Wheel.

We can sleep on the beach, he says. Up by the rocks. It's just for a few hours. In the morning we can hire a car. Drive into the mountains.

Making a bed out of rucksacks and jumpers and Luke's leather coat. Luke places his pocket knife under their makeshift pillow. Cuddling up, swigging duty-free tequila.

Woods burns with a sound like ice cracking. Fire on the beach. The whistle of a burning log, for a moment, the loudest sound and the flames, apricot, pale orange in the centre with kicks of blue.

Do you think Joe will be very hurt that we stole his money?

What do you care?

Pia says: I don't want Joe to hate me.

He's just a punter, Luke says

Joe cannot let them go.

Feeling trapped now inside this room, sitting on the bed beside Helen.

She has not stopped speaking since they left, a monotonous monologue – and, every so often those words (and always with a wistfulness) the Spanish Steps.

He has stopped saying: we can still go.

Wanting only to say now: be quiet.

He knows that she is hurting and that he is the cause of it, he knows that she is his wife and his attention should be with her, but it fled with the two of them leaving. Like they took the biggest part of him with them.

Got to go, he says.

What are you talking about?

Got to find them.

Why?

Joe has jumped up from the bed, he is hurriedly assembling things in his pockets from his drawers.

Can't explain it.

His words like his movements are fast and jerky.

Got to go now.

Emptying the bedside drawer onto the bed, discarding coins and elastic bands, a packet of cigarettes, handkerchiefs, a bottle of cologne.

Have you seen it?

What?

My envelope of currency, says Joe. Have you seen it?

No.

Transparent envelope. Joe starts describing it to her and all the time he is emptying his pockets on to the bed and checking and rechecking.

Blue writing on it, about this big – making an oblong with his hands.

No.

It had almost everything I had inside of it. Have you seen it?

Framed in the doorway, still frantically searching his pockets. Wanting only to get out of here and Helen is laughing. A false, high sound that shrills in the air.

I guess you do have to go after them, she sneers. You or the police. Your friends are criminals – she is still laughing. A couple of thieves.

Joe has been walking half the night when he sees them. Curled up together on the rocks, coat pulled over them.

Joe knew he would find them. Not meant to lose Pia. Of that he is certain. Pulled towards her. It is as if she holds the only light. And the world in darkness.

Had to come after her.

Couldn't explain to Helen. How to make her understand? Can't understand it himself. Got to, got to be with her.

Joe stays watching them for so long, crouching on the rocks, that his legs go numb. Unable to move.

It is as if they are separated behind glass.

It is as if he is a man in a cinema hall watching an unmoving image – an image he could break with a movement of his hand, like rippling the surface of a pool.

So still in the silence, waiting for them to wake.

It is something about the way they are lying. As the sun begins to come up. Looking at them, noticing. Not sure what it is. Her leg over his leg, his arm behind her head. Not like brother and sister. Not just that.

Watching them stir slowly. Stretching out in the weak light. Stretching and then curling in towards each other.

A cuddle. Nothing more than that. And yet.

The feeling – the kicking low in his gut – that he has begun to associate with them. Rising now from his chest and throat.

That edginess – thinks Joe – that sits between them like still air – like still air before the beating of wings. Of course a sister is going to love her brother but all the time – he knew it – there was something else. The millisecond before an explosion.

Joe feels he will throw up.

Behind the rocks, so close to them but hidden. Tearing a cry from his throat.

Pia and Luke hear Joe's voice – so close, but it seems to come from a distance. They draw in closer together.

Stepping out from behind the rocks, the rocks which seem to be shifting. Joe holds his head in his hands until the rocks grow still again. Then he looks up at Pia.

She is looking at and through him again.

Always pushing him away. Lost her to Luke – before he started – a foregone conclusion.

The knowledge comes with an anger, a swift, sweeping anger that takes him close to Luke, fist clenched tight.

And Pia is rushing at Joe. Screaming at him. Seeming to come at him from a long distance.

Feeling him suddenly near and his hair is in her fingers knotted in there pulling his head backwards.

Pia sees Joe's eyes: two rings of intense white around two circles of intense black. As Pia looks at them the white becomes whiter and the black blacker. The more Pia stares into them the bigger they grow until they reach the size of the earth.

The pocket knife is in Pia's hand and as Joe moves – his mouth has grown bigger and his lips keep opening and closing, chest heaving up and down – she lifts it and buries it deep in Joe's neck.

Holding on, clawing and screaming, Luke somewhere beneath them. The choking sound of breath.

Pia.

What is he trying to say?

Pushing him away, the knife in her hand.

Pia.

Pia pulls the knife out of Joe's neck and thrusts it deep in his chest, pulls it out of his chest and plunges it into his belly.

Pia sticks the knife into almost every part of Joe's body.

Her hand moves easily as she thrusts the knife into his flesh and pulls it out.

Almost without effort.

Suddenly still now. Around her only blackness. Then slowly the crash of a wave on the rocks around her. The crash and crash of a wave.

Catching Shellfish Between the Tides

ROSALYN CHISSICK

Stories change lives. That is their purpose.

Magda is twelve years old. She has silver bangles up to her elbows and on her left shoulder a tattoo of the moon. She is searching for the life she never had.

Reality and fantasy blur, reflecting Magda's increasingly fragmented mind, as she tells story after story – of the baby daughter she calls Missing because she knows she will lose her, of the mother she selected in a supermarket, and of the man who inspires Magda to change her stories, and so change her life.

A winner of prizes before it was published, *Catching Shellfish between the Tides* is a hauntingly vivid, lyrical and sensual first novel about the history and dreams of a young woman and the vital role that storytelling plays in all our lives.

∫

SCEPTRE

A selection of other books from
Sceptre

The Crime of Olga Arbyelina	Andrëi Maxine	0 340 72315 9	£6.99 ☐
The Nanny and the Iceberg	Ariel Dorfman	0 340 71303 8	£6.99 ☐
Gorgeous	Lynne Bryan	0 340 73969 X	£6.99 ☐
Self-Portrait with Ghosts	Kelly Dwyer	0 340 73948 7	£6.99 ☐
Cold Mountain	Charles Frazier	0 340 68059 8	£6.99 ☐

All Sceptre books are available from your local bookshop or newsagent, or can be ordered direct from the publisher. Just tick the titles you want and fill in the form below. Prices and availability subject to change without notice.

Hodder & Stoughton Books, Cash Sales Department, Bookpoint, 39 Milton Park, Abingdon, OXON, OX14 4TD, UK. E-mail address: order@bookpoint.co.uk. If you have a credit card you may order by telephone – (01235) 400414.

Please enclose a cheque or postal order made payable to Bookpoint Ltd to the value of the cover price and allow the following for postage and packing:
UK & BFPO – £1.00 for the first book, 50p for the second book, and 30p for each additional book ordered up to a maximum charge of £3.00.
OVERSEAS & EIRE – £2.00 for the first book, £1.00 for the second book, and 50p for each additional book

Name _____

Address _____

_____

_____

If you would prefer to pay by credit card, please complete:
Please debit my Visa/Access/Diner's Card/American Express (delete as applicable) card no:

Signature _____

Expiry Date _____

If you would NOT like to receive further information on our products please tick the box. ☐